SECRET TENNESSEE

By

Beverly A. Morris

Tanya!
(Cup Cakes Momma)
Thank You for your
Support.

Beverly A. Morris
10/13/2012

This book is a work of fiction. Names, characters, places, and incidents are either the product of the author's imagination or are used fictitiously, and any resemblance to actual persons, living or dead, business establishments, events, or locales is entirely coincidental.

Cover design by Larry Norman
Editorial support and book layout by DBePub.com.
ISBN: 978-0-9859722-0-2

DEDICATION

For Morgan & Megan

This book is dedicated to all of the special people in my life who have believed in me and encouraged me to write. These include my big brother Larry and some of my best friends, like Beechnut, Sara, and my dear Janice. I send a special tribute to my number one fan, Sharon, and, last but not least, Roger. God bless all of you!

TO THE READER

In this book, I'll take you on a journey where you'll meet some people that you just might think you know. There are so many people, places, and things, some so familiar... know what I mean? Well, I say, if the shoe fits, wear it, and that's all right here in *Secret Tennessee.*

In Webster's, the definition of the secret is (1) *concealed or hidden from sight,* (2) *kept from the knowledge or view of those concerned.* But here in Tennessee, we take "secret" to a whole new level. Here it means concealed or hidden *no matter what*!

Now I'm sure, no matter where you come from, you've got secrets there. How often have you heard, "Don't say nothing to nobody; it's a secret"? Michael Franks sings a song, "Your Secret's Safe with Me," and, in AA, they say, "You're only as sick as your secrets." Sure, every place has secrets, but *this* place! Well, this whole place is made of secrets and, if you don't have any, you just ain't from here.

Around here, even if you want to tell, you better think twice. Here there's a rule that's taught to all of us. In fact, here in Tennessee, this rule is practically law. (If you don't know this law, then, again, clearly, you ain't from around here!) The thing is, here, even when you want to tell, you can't because they've been teaching you from the time you could talk, "Keep it hush-hush." "Don't tell nobody your business." "Keep quiet, that's family business." Around here, a kid might even get his butt whipped if he tells the wrong thing.

So many things in this little town are, as they call it nowadays, "on the down low." Kids, old folks, preachers, teachers, police, judges, salesmen, they're all keeping secrets. And if you tell a secret, they'll call you a snitch, and you know what they say about snitches:

Snitches get stitches.

VALERIE

I've been principal of this elementary school now for the last eight years. People say I've got this under control. I'm told all the time by parents that they want their kid to go to my school. And why not? We score highest in all academics, sports, creative and performing arts. I've got good morals and I believe in keeping children respectful. Parents like that.

That doesn't stop the talk. I heard some parents talking when I passed by them in the auditorium on graduation day. Some big-haired woman said, "Wonder where she went to school. I heard it was some school in the hood."

"South Memphis?" another one guessed.

"No, Box-town." Some man leaned up from two rows back to add his two cents.

"Well, I just can't tell. She seems so put together all the time," Big-Hair added.

Yeah, I got it all together, but sometimes, wow, I'm just so glad the day is over. Some of these damn kids need their ass whipped and so do some of these parents. When I was coming up you didn't get to ask questions, you just did it!

What these people don't know is I danced my ass off to pay for my college degree. Night after night, waiting tables, rushing to get the next trick coming in the door. I got sick of smiling and acting sexy each and every night. I hated it! But I told myself, "Soon, one day soon, it will be over." When I got so tired I didn't think I could take it, I'd chant, "How long? Not long."

Looking back now, of course, it paid off and no one was the wiser. Until recently, I just thanked God that I'd never run into one of my old customers. If these parents only knew where I really came from, how I really grew up! But no one knows my secret except…well... he said he'd never tell.

It was Thursday evening, it finally happened. Out of all the people I've met and all the places I've been, it was a damn basketball banquet. We had this end-of-the-school-year program to honor our basketball coach, Tommy Wilkerson. He's been a good coach, so we had this program for him, and, of course, he'd want his father with him, right? Well, after I made my closing remarks, I noticed this old man staring at me. Just like that, after not seeing it for so long, it was like I was back there. I knew that look all right, because, for a long time, that look meant money. I sort of ignored it, told myself it was nothing, because, I confess, sometimes I have a tendency to get a bit paranoid, thinking that someone will one day show up from my past and tell my secret. Well, turns out I wasn't just being paranoid this time.

When everyone started leaving the auditorium, he came closer to me, even though he's old now and can hardly get around. He came right up close enough to whisper in my ear.

I felt his hot breath on my face and I swear a little spit hit my cheek. "I remember you, little lady. It's been twenty-five years, but I remember. You used to put on quite a show. What was that name you used? Hmm…? Spider, that's it."

"Spider," he said softer, huskier.

I took a step away, trying not to wrinkle my nose at the old man smell of him, putting on my professional principal face. "You must have me mixed up with someone else."

He shook his head. "No…no... I would never forget that face. Or that body. I may be old, but there are some things a man just doesn't forget. But, don't worry, I won't tell. You were a good time for me. The way I see it, you deserve a good life."

About that time Coach Wilkerson walked up. "I see you've met my dad. Be careful. He can be a handful."

I smiled at Coach. "Yes! He's quite a guy. Congratulations, again, Coach. Great year."Fortunately, everybody knew I was headed out to Nashville the next morning for a conference, so I had a good excuse to high-tail it out of there.

The next night I was enjoying the perks of being forced to attend one more in an endless stream of professional development conferences. The rest of the weekend might be a struggle to either stay awake or keep from strangling some long-winded ass, but tonight I got to sit with a nice glass of Chardonnay in a Jacuzzi, anticipating fine linens and feather pillows and enough AC to need the complementary extra quilt I had sent up with my bags.

School principals from all over Tennessee attend this one: high school, middle school, elementary school, private schools and charter schools, even the Catholic school principals. They were all here. The keynote speaker was some university professor coming from Chattanooga. I only hoped he didn't think a chair in the education department meant his speech needed to take forever. I had already checked the schedule to see how early I could get away for my yearly shopping spree at the outlet malls.

The hotel is beautiful. They'd done some remodeling since last year, so it was even nicer now. Didn't stop me from giving the bathroom a once over with my own Lysol. Can't be too careful, but in a hotel like this, hey, it might not even have needed it. Especially since everything stays so nice and cool all the time. In here, even though it's hot as hell outside, you forget all about the weather. You even get cold most times in the meetings and all. I paused with the wine halfway to my mouth to think if I remembered my sweater. Shrug. Whatever, I can buy one in the gift shop if I need it, and maybe pick up some nice candles to put around the tub tomorrow night, too.

This hotel always feels like California to me. The lobby is like a nice day in Los Angeles with the temperature just right. The place is huge, with indoor gardens and waterfalls. They have palm trees blowing in the breeze of over-sized fans, and skylights make you feel like you're outside. Some of the rooms on the upper floors have a patio where you can sit overlooking an inner courtyard to watch people checking in. In the morning, I'll sit out there on my patio, with a cup of Starbucks, reading *USA Today*. I'll check my email, Twitter, and Facebook on my iPad and feel like, wow, I've come a long way from the nights of eating top ramen noodles before taping up the heel on my cheap shoes and going out on stage to dance all night.

I smiled at that thought and climbed out of the Jacuzzi before I got too pruney. Early day tomorrow if I was going to get my slow cup of coffee before breakfast and the plenary session at nine a.m.

Let's see, right after the plenary was a thing called *Making Sure You Know Your School's History* by an acquaintance at a rival school, so I wanted to go see how she would do with that. Then there was a workshop that actually looked slightly interesting, *Monitoring, Handling, and Recognizing Gang Violence at your School.* I was mostly just curious, because the speaker wasn't African American. Not that only African Americans are in gangs. I was wondering how he'd approach the topic. That would get me to lunch, anyway.

I got there right on time, grabbed me one of them nice looking cheese Danishes and another half a cup of coffee, and found me a comfortable seat in the middle of the auditorium, but on the aisle. Easy access to the door if the speaker was too dull, and I decided that my phone just suddenly vibrated and I needed to duck out to take an important call. Throughout my entire school attendance, I've always chosen a seat in the middle. Never liked to sit at the very front or the very end of anywhere. I'm always in the middle of any class or seminar. Guess I'm just a middle of the road kind of girl.

People were trickling in, and at about ten after, the hotel actually brought in fresh coffee. So, it was going to be that kind of conference, the kind that starts late and never catches up. Sigh.

By nine fifteen, most people were finally seated and the speaker was on the dais. A few late arrivals came scuttling in as one of the organizers handed the speaker a glass of water and the monitors started to close the doors. I looked around. They were a pretty motley bunch. A few of the latecomers still had wet hair. One was definitely out of breath. More than a few looked like they just fell out of bed. A couple with matching red dye jobs looked like they just fell out of a bar. Then, this lady pushed in the already closed door, "Excuse me, sorry, excuse me."

She shuffled up to me, motioning she wanted in the row. "Excuse me. Sorry." I'm thinking, why didn't she stay in the back? Why pick my row? But, she insisted on climbing over me to get to the seat next to me. She was completely disheveled, hair looking kind of wild.

Then this bitch knocked over my CrocoItalian leather briefcase with her Jack Georges Ostrich one. Even with papers hanging all out of it, it was fine. I thought I had it going on until I saw hers. Damn. That shit cost about three grand and she couldn't even be bothered to straighten up the papers in it before she closed it. Everybody was looking at her and she just kept saying, "Excuse me. Excuse me," while she bumped me, the lady on her other side, and, I'm pretty sure, the lady in front of her, too.

Finally, she plopped down next to me, knocking my elbow one more time, looked right at me, and said with a big smile, "Good morning. I almost overslept!"

That's when I heard her voice, I mean really heard it. There is only one voice like that in the world. Diamond. I looked past her Jack Georges to her face. Oh my God, it was her, the Quaalude queen, Diamond, in the flesh. I couldn't believe it! Still white as a sheet, still wild looking, same schoolgirl figure, same hairstyle, and those red freckles all over her face. After all these years, still the same. I whispered, "Diamond?"

She looked at me. "Spider!"

Then the person next to us shushed us and the emcee started welcoming everyone. I smiled at Diamond, thinking this conference just got interesting.

She whispered back. "Oh, my Lord, Spider."

I extended my hand, very formal. "Valerie Chatman."

She shook my hand. "Melissa Phinella. Pleased to meet you."We both smiled and then looked away before we could start laughing.

As soon as the illustrious professor started droning on, I knew by the mutual eye rolls and sighs that me and Diamond - Melissa - both wanted to duck out of there and go catch up, but late participants filled in the back of the room and pretty quickly we were trapped there. What'd they do, get a room half the size they needed?

I thought that man would never stop talking. He went on and on, and Melissa even nudged me once when I started to nod off. By the time I thought he might finally finish, I knew I wanted to run up to my room at the break. No way was I waiting down here in this crowd to pee. In case we got separated for the next session, I wrote my room number on the back of a business card and passed it to Melissa, 441. She gave me hers, room 443. How about that? We were just across the hall from each other. Small world. We made a quick plan to go to dinner together, and as soon as the guy started taking questions, I moved to muscle past the crowd and out the door.

Diamond and I had arranged to meet at the Solario at eight, leaving me time for a power nap. With a nap on the horizon and dinner with Diamond, the evening suddenly seemed a lot more promising.

I woke to the blip of my phone, a text message from Diamond. "We still on?"

I got up, found my glasses, and responded, "Absolutely. Give me ten. And it's my treat."

A quick shower, my one black dress, and I was out the door. Diamond was already halfway through the first pitcher of margaritas when I get there. She had chips and salsa and a salted glass for me. It was going to be a good night.

She poured me a drink. "I am so glad this day is over. Did you hear one interesting thing today?"

I didn't even have to think. "Not really. Let's forget that; let's catch up, girl. Wow, how long has it been?"

"Well, I'm fifty-five. I was twenty then. You do the math."

"Girl, it's a wonder we're alive. All the crazy shit we did back then. And saw, too, right?"

"Yeah!" she said, "Remember that 'special' stripper? The main attraction? She had to be two hundred fifty pounds. Big everything. And so many men came to see her. Now, you knew, right? She was really a man!"

We fell out laughing. We were so naïve back then, and we thought we had it going on. "You know, that's nothing nowadays, but back then, I had no idea!"

"Girl, you're crazy."

"You ever see her naked? No, you didn't, did you? I promise you, she was a man."

I just shook my head and took another long drink. I caught the eye of the bartender so he'd send over another pitcher. "You remember that old police officer who used to come in and stay all day. What kind of police was that? And he would be staggering drunk when he left. What precinct could he have worked at? He wouldn't get away with that shit nowadays. His ass would've been all over the news."

"Yeah! Remember one time he got so drunk he took out his little junk and got on stage with one of the girls. Who was it? I don't remember. I just remember him dancing, waving around that little bitty ole thing."

"Yeah, I kinda remember that, but the part I really remember is him leaving his wallet on the table, and when I came to his table with another drink and he was on stage acting a fool, I just politely opened his wallet and got me six of the ten hundred-dollar bills he had in there. When he got back to his table, he says to me, 'Come here, Motherfucker.' He always called everybody motherfucker. He paid his tab and gave me a twenty-dollar tip and he never missed a dollar. I wonder what he thought happened when he sobered up the next day."

We were having a good time. I had a good buzz on, then Diamond had to bring up the bad night.

"You remember," she said more quietly," that poor little hick red-headed girl, the one who looked like she just came out of the cornfield? What was her name? We called her Little Red…. She looked like Granny from the Beverly Hillbillies. Remember that night her mother came in looking for her?"

"Yeah, I remember. Her momma found out she was dancing and tried to make her quit. I was there when the bouncer told her momma she had to leave. That poor woman was crying and crying, saying, 'That's my baby in there.' Poor Jackson, I know he felt bad. He kept saying 'I'm sorry, ma'am, but she's eighteen. If she don't want to go home with you, you can't make her. ' He finally told her she had to leave because she was distracting the dancers and bothering the customers."

"I know. I was in the dressing room with Red when her mother tried to get her to go. She begged her, but Red just told her to get out. Told her mother she was trying to make some money."

"Did you hear the shot?"

"I didn't. I don't know why I didn't, but all I knew was, suddenly, there were cops everywhere. Gosh, what a horrible way to go. And poor Little Red, she must still be carrying that guilt, right? Having her mother shoot herself right there on the back steps."

"I don't know. I never saw that girl again, did you?"

She just shook her head, and I was glad for the tequila.

"That was so sad."

We sat there bummed for a minute in silence, then shook it off.

She said, "You know, it could've been worse, working there. Anything could've happened to us, but that's about the only bad thing I remember."

I raised a glass."To things not being worse."

Melissa filled me in on some of her history, "I worked out in Millington for a while. I remember this man got shot in the head by some young drug dealer. Happened while I was on stage. His brains splattered all over my feet and costume. I was in shock. I will never forget the shoes I had on. They were black patent leather trimmed in gold. I paid a hundred twenty dollars for those shoes. They were one of my favorite money making shoes. That was a lot of money for a pair of shoes back in our day. After that ordeal, I think I worked about another week and that was when I ended my dancing career.

"The rest was all about making money to pay for tuition and having a good time. I hear it's really different now. They've got gang bangers, big time ballers, girls that try to pimp girls, meth and crack addicts, lesbians, and I hear the girls dancing now really, really work hard for their money. We were talked bad about for dancing topless, but now that's a joke. You can't get a dime now for dancing like we did then. Girls these days go completely nude. They get pennies thrown at them if the customers think they're ugly or can't dance.

If they look like a drug addict they get cursed out and called all kinds of names. Spider, God was looking out for us."

"Yeah," I said, "You know they say He takes care of babies and fools. Waiter. Waiter. Excuse me. Could you bring us another pitcher? This time strawberry margarita."

"Coming right up," he answered.

"Okay. What are you having to eat? These margaritas are starting to creep up on me."

"Let's see. I think I'll have taco salad," I answered.

"And I'll have the chicken enchiladas."

We ate and drank and laughed and talked about all of the twists and turns life had brought us. We had a great time talking and laughing about the past, and when I checked my watch, it was ten p.m. If we were gonna make the morning session on time, we'd better get some sleep.

After a full day of presentations, Saturday's meeting culminated in a banquet. There was a nice surprise for me, a special recognition for my work.

After the banquet I turned to Melissa. "Okay, girl. Now we are going to take this party a step further and go down memory lane. I just called the concierge's desk and arranged a cab for nine o'clock tonight."

"What! Where are we going? No. No. Don't tell me."

"I've got it all planned. I did my homework and I found a place that should be pretty safe for us to go to. Meet me in the lobby at seven forty-five."

"Wait," Melissa said, "What should I wear?"

"Whatever you like, but be sure it's something sexy."

EVA

Next Sunday was going to be the celebration for the pastor and his wife's anniversary. I decided I just had to find out what color they would be wearing. There is no way I was going to let her look better than me. I'm the one who really deserves to be with him! I'm the one he runs to after a stressful week at work, a hard night after weekly Bible study, revivals, and three Sunday services.

Every time I see her walk in with him, my stomach just turns and balls up in knots. Feels like I've been eating a bag of Hot Cheetos. You know, those chips that all the teenagers eat?

I've been in this church for years, singing in the choir. You'd think she'd get it by now. It's getting harder and harder to not show how I really feel about the pastor. But if I ever let it out, or tell a single soul, he promised he'd be done with me. I just love him too much to ever take that chance. Plus, it would crush William. He's one of the pastor's lead deacons. I know. I'll call my sister, Lorraine, the pastor's secretary. I know how to talk to her, and eventually she'll let it slip out in our conversation. I think I'll call her tomorrow.

Well, let's see. When and how did it all get started? It was one Sunday back in, well, quite a few years back. My husband and I and the kids had attended Sunday Service there several times as guests of my big sister. This particular Sunday, something touched my heart and I said," Honey, let's join today. We need a church home. You know this is the kind of church I'm accustomed to. My granddaddy, daddy and mom were all raised and brought all of us up to be Church of God in Christ. This feels right, and I think this is where the Lord wants us to be."

So we joined, and the pastor said these words, "Make me a good member, and I'll make you a good pastor." But there was something about the look in his eye and that handshake that said something more.

My husband is a good, kind, God-fearing man. I love him more than life itself. We have two beautiful children, a son and daughter. But when he was only thirty-seven, my husband was diagnosed with prostate cancer, and after he had the surgery, the sex went out the window. Oh, we tried everything—Viagra, Cialis, Levitra, the pump—and nothing, nothing, worked. I've became so, so frustrated. He's bought me toys. They worked for a while, but…don't let nobody tell you that works forever, 'cause, as Marvin Gaye and Tammy Terrell told us long ago, "Ain't nothing like the real thing."

The only person I've confided in is my friend, Jessica. She's about my age, and she's divorced. I felt like maybe she could understand what I'm going through. She's been real sweet to me, but she keeps encouraging me to join this book club of hers. I just don't feel like a book club is going to help me that much.

Last February was the straw that broke the camel's back. I'd been enduring this no sex thing for three years. We went to Sausalito, California for Valentines Day, and we stayed at this elegant place called the Casa Madrona. I'd been planning this trip all year, and our suite was the most romantic place I'd ever been in my entire life. Fireplace, feather bed, ocean view, Egyptian silk sheets, champagne and truffles. What more could a girl ask for? I was so glad my sister had volunteered to keep the kids. I knew they were getting the proper care, 'cause she's pretty strict. They wouldn't be able to run over her like they do with my niece when she watches them. I was so proud of how I'd planned the entire trip. The flight, hotel, and the ferry from San Francisco were just right. I've always been great at getting the best for less.

But what a letdown! We had five days together. No kids, no fights or arguments to settle, no phones ringing, no dog barking, bird chirping, just perfect; just the two of us. We had dinner at this romantic restaurant, with a bottle of my favorite wine. Afterwards, we walked along the street, hand in hand, looking out at all the boats on the dock all the way back to our suite. I'd brought all of my favorites with me: body butter from Europe, foot massage cream, hazelnut soy candles, KY warming gel, and of course, my special toys. I wore his favorite black sexy nighty with my fishnet stockings and black patent leather stilettos. My iPod was loaded with all of my favorite music. I even brought whipped cream and honey butter. Will Downing was singing *The Look of Love*, my husband was massaging me from head to toe, and, oh, it felt so damn good. Just as good as sucking on a milk chocolate truffle! Whew! He knew how and where to rub and I knew just what to do for him, too.

Except, when we got to the final lovemaking moment, all there was, was, emptiness. Nothing! Just lifeless, no life at all. He cried and so did I.

I loved him so, so, much, but there was no use in trying anymore. I had to face facts. At thirty-five years old I would no longer be able to make love to my husband. I knew then I'd never leave him, but a young woman has needs, and somehow I had to find a way to fulfill them without hurting anyone. We made the best of our trip, and he showered me with gifts and allowed me to purchase all kinds of beautiful things at all my favorite places to compensate for the lack of sex. I bought shoes and suits at Nordstrom and Saks. I went to the Farmers Market, where I hand picked fruit and had it shipped home. Then a few specialty stores where I purchased some items like a pearl necklace and earring set, a new gold broach, perfume, and a few outfits for the kids. I spent a quick ten grand. I loved him so much, and I hated the hand that life had dealt him, but I realized that this was the way it was, and it was never going to change. I just had to learn to live with it.

We flew back in the afternoon, and got home around six p.m. on Saturday evening. I had made arrangements for the limo service to pick up the kids after they picked us up from the airport, and on the way home from my sister's house I gave everyone their souvenirs from our trip. I knew they'd get a kick out of it.

Lorraine called while I was unpacking. "Are ya'll gonna make service tomorrow?"

"I am really tired, but we'll be there, girl. Anything special going on?

"No, just checking. I don't want ya'll to miss out on your blessing." That sister of mine loves the Lord, and Pastor Clarke. She takes her job as church secretary seriously.

The service was great, and the pastor kept saying, "God's got a blessing with your name on it."

He spoke from the book of Matthew, Chapter 4: 12-16. After service I went up to thank the pastor and told him how much I enjoyed the service. He gave me a warm clasp of his hand. "Thank you, Sister Halston."

I had forgotten that today was the last show for the Unisoul Circus, and we had promised the kids that they could go. I was still feeling exhausted from the trip, and I told my husband to go on without me. I didn't want to spoil the kids' day. He agreed and said, "How will you get home?"

I said, "I'll catch a ride with my sister."

When I went to look for Lorraine, she had already left, so the pastor volunteered to take me home. He assured me, "Sister Halston, I don't mind. It's not too far out of my way. I'll be happy to drop you off."

"I hate to be a bother to you."

"No problem."

He directed me out the church to his car. I was surprised he wasn't driving a Cadillac. What a gentleman he was; he opened the car door for me and I slid in.

We rode part way home in silence, just the music playing from 95.7. There was a gospel song playing called *God Didn't Give up on Me.* Pastor looked over at me. "Can I say this to you, sister? I feel like you've been carrying a burden. Seems as if something is weighing heavy on your heart. Anything you wish to share with me?"

"I'm okay... my husband and I just got back from a wonderful trip to Sausalito, California, and we had a great time. It was our anniversary."

"Then why the sadness?"

Before I knew it, I broke out in tears. Soon the whole story poured out of me, my husband's impotence and how I'd been faithful throughout our entire marriage. How I was so frustrated and how I didn't know what to do! He helped me in the house and he said, "Let me pray for you."

He held my hands together. My God, he has such soft hands. Then he touched my head and put my head in between his hands. He touched my heart…well, chest…well, breast, really. That's when I melted. The next thing I knew we were kissing and hugging and rubbing and, then, the clothes started coming off. Oh, he smelled so good. I think it was Ralph Lauren Blue for

Men. I thought, "Didn't smell that good on my husband, or maybe I'm just hot."

A song by Jill Scott flashed through my head about how that cologne smelled good on you but stunk on him. First he kissed my breasts, one at a time, slowly. Then he rubbed everywhere. Then he kneeled down as if praying, and I lost my mind. Forgot I was in my own home. Forgot he was the pastor. Forgot I was married. Everything. I hadn't felt this damn good in such a longtime! Then his pants went down and, there, before me, stood this long, long, beautiful, hard...

I closed my eyes and left earth for a while.

It's been going on every since that Sunday, and I don't know if I can keep up this secret any longer. I find myself obsessing over him, wondering what he's doing, and fighting not to call his home or cell phone or send him a text message. I know that just wouldn't be right, but I can't seem to help myself. I have fallen in love with him.

I don't think anyone knows, and of course that's how it has to be. I'd never hurt William. But my heart is hurting, and I don't know what to do. Every time we get together we say that it's wrong, that it will be our last time, but something happens and we end up back in bed together again. He has a wife that loves him, and I have a husband who truly loves me.

Somehow, someway, this has got to stop before our secret gets out. But as the song says," If loving you is wrong, I don't wanna be right!" How in the hell did I get myself in this mess? I know my husband doesn't deserve this, and I know Sister Clarke doesn't either.

DANA

I can still see her lying there in that casket, her blond hair shot through with white, and those soft blue eyes closed forever. She died and never told a soul, but now that she's gone, I'm telling. I never would have told. I never told anything that she made me promise not to. But I'm telling now. I never really understood how a person could keep a secret and take it all the way to the grave. Even on her last days, when I came to see her, she reminded me that some things are just best left a secret. She never wanted the neighbors or any of her girlfriends to know just what form of cancer she had, and I promised never to tell. Every time I pass that hospital, and especially when I drive by Memorial Park Cemetery, I remember her. How can I ever forget? I remember her saying," I'm ready to go. I'm tired and just plain old ready to go home."

When she was in the hospital, Mommy could track me like a FedEx package. She made good use of her Mother's Day present from me, that damn cell phone. She called that last afternoon and asked, "Dana, are you at the funeral home yet? How much do they want for that pink casket? Eighteen thousand! Oh, no, that's too damn much. Just get me the cheapest one that you can, and find me a pink gown, since I can't afford that pink casket. I wish someone would bring me a cigarette. I feel every grown person ought to be able to do whatever they want. If I want to smoke and I have cancer, so what... I can. My goodness, it's not going to change a single thing now, anyway. Well, I'm tired and I'm ready to go home. Not the one on Canton Street, but the home away from this earth."

"Oh, Mommy," I sighed, "you're going home. To your very own house on Canton Street."

"No, Baby, I'm going to my real home to meet the Lord. You know. Glory."

"Okay, Mommy, I'll talk to you later. I am getting ready to go out to the mall and find you the perfect pink gown."

"Good, that's my girl, Dana. See you later."

Wow, my mommy is really, really gone. She knew her last days were near and that last night when I went to see her she said, "Dana, don't come here tomorrow, 'cause I'll be gone."

"Sure, Mommy. I'll see you same time tomorrow, ten a.m."

When I got there and walked in the room, the nurse was dialing my cell number. She had passed away at nine fifty-eight a.m. I loved her so much and I will miss her forever. My mommy was a tough cookie, and she protected us just like a mother bird protects her babies.

I'm grateful to have had these last few months, taking care of Mommy, even though it's been so hard. I've had to take time away from my job as a school librarian. Fortunately, my principal has been really supportive. Valerie and I have become friends through this process. I don't know her that well; she's always been one of those people who keep to herself. It doesn't seem like she has many friends, outside of a book club I heard her mention once when she was on the phone.

I knew the hard part was coming now. I'd have to deal with my greedy sisters. Mommy didn't have much, but those two would fight over what she had anyway. They weren't around when we could have used their help, but they'd sure be in line to see what they could get.

When it was six months from the day we buried our mother, I knew it was time to settle a few things. I could stand to wait at least a year, but my sisters were sure there must have been some kind of insurance policy, and they wouldn't let up about it or leave me alone. This was the most they have ever stayed in touch with me. I found her will, which spelled out who got what for the three of us. I couldn't believe she left them everything! Those two sisters of mine, who never spent much time with Mommy throughout her illness, didn't give a hoot about helping buy her medicine, or take time to listen to her last request before dying, walked away with almost everything she had.

She did leave the house to my niece, Julie, her one and only granddaughter. Thank God, because Julie's mother would have sold it. She left the car and all of her jewelry to Dianne, and all of the antique furniture and silver to Debbie, and the little money that was left in her bank account, all of $9,075, she split between them.

And you know what she left me? Nothing. Just two boxes of old family pictures and a lot of old papers. She said she knew I would be the best one to have them. She knew I would take them and put them in proper photo albums like she wanted to do, but never got around to. So I took the two boxes and left. My sisters were sitting outside of the house, glad that was all she left me.

"See, I'm not her favorite," I said, "Just the oldest."

While driving back home, I had time to think and reflect back on all the memories of times we had together. How, every Valentines Day, she would give us all a box of candy and new pretty underwear, usually pink or red, and, every Halloween, she would make caramel apples and Granny Smith apples for bobbing. We'd wear homemade Halloween costumes. She would always crochet a new blanket or throw cover for each of us at Christmas. We had an Easter egg hunt and invited everyone from the church to hunt for eggs. She always had one special golden egg and all of us worked hard to find that one. She would always give us a hint where it would be. It always had money inside and as we got older, the amount of money would get bigger.

I remembered as I was driving how she used to take us to Whiteville to visit her sister. We would stay two weeks with our twin cousins every summer while school was out. We got to know Mommy's two sisters. My mother had one brother, but she never, ever, ever, let us get to know him. That was her big brother, our Uncle Walter Eisenberg, who lived in Dresden. Mommy said he was no good. She hated him. I never knew why. What had he done so bad to make her hate him? The only uncle that we knew of in our entire family.

We never got to know any of my daddy's people at all. When dad left, he left. Never heard a word from him. He paid his child support, but he never called or came around. I don't know if Mommy fixed it that way, or he just didn't want to be bothered.

It was almost dark when I arrived home. I took the boxes in the house and sat them on the kitchen window seat, one of my favorite places in this house. I decided I'd go through them in the morning when I got up and had my coffee. I was exhausted, sad, confused, hurt and angry.

But early the next morning, my curiosity took over. Mommy must have had these boxes for decades. They were dusty and smelled like old people. They were filled with pictures, ticket stubs, and all kinds of papers. Newspaper articles, obituaries, church programs, graduation announcements. I even found my 5th grade report card. All kinds of pictures, one in particular in which I'd felt really beautiful, and on the back it said Dana, age 16. I found a picture of Debbie and Dianne as newborn babies held by some man and woman. The picture was old and in black and white. Some pieces were falling apart, and on the back it said, "Debbie and Dianne at six months."

She had a picture of herself. Oh, my God, she was so beautiful, pretty blonde hair hanging down her back and a mole on her face right beside her lip. And, oh, my God, she had dimples. I'd never seen her dimples. She hardly ever smiled. Hmm… I didn't remember ever seeing the mole on Mommy's face, but I guess that was the style then. On the back of that picture, it said age 24. I kept digging, and near the bottom of the box I saw a little black coin purse. They don't make this kind anymore. Inside it was one key. I thought to myself, "Wonder what this key goes to?"

I stopped for a minute and went to get another cup of coffee. Then I started going through some of the papers. I found one peculiar looking form. It was old and yellow, rolled up with a rubber band that had just about dried up. Legal documents from The Probate Court of Shelby County, Tennessee, finalizing the adoption of Debbie and Dianne Eisenberg by Cherry and Robert Davis. Docket A-7356.

I was in shock. I never knew, never knew about this. My two sisters are really not my sisters. They are really my cousins. I never had a clue. No wonder we never saw eye to eye. We never liked the same clothes, shoes, hairstyles, music, food or boys. They came from someplace else. Not the same blood. Well, kind of, but not really.

My sisters actually belonged to my mother's brother. Seems he was declared an unfit father. There were accusations of drinking problems, giving the children beer in bottles instead of milk, and he was a registered sex offender.

In the petition, it stated that the children were found walking around unclothed and unbathed. So, oh my God! I wonder what happened to their mother. As I read further, I learned Cora Eisenberg was incarcerated for murder and sentenced to life at the Hardeman County CCA. My God, how would I ever be able to look at them and not say a word?

VALERIE

It took us twenty-five minutes to get to Déjà Vu and, on a Saturday night, it was packed. We looked at each other, smiled, and said in unison, "Let's do the damned thang."

That's what we used to say before we would go on stage in the old days. "Oh my God, girl, look at these chicks," I said, "In our day you only had one white and one black girl with a boob job. Here they all fucking got them."

The place was set up nice. Long bar with granite counter top. Nice sconces on the wall and everything inside this place was in the color purple. They even have someone check and wand you down before you get in to make sure you don't come up in here with any weapons.

"Now, where in the hell do we sit?" Melissa asked.

Before I could say a word, this young girl came and said, "Follow me. I have the perfect seats for you two."

I thought, "Oh damn! They think we are a couple. Well, what the hell? They don't know us anyway."

They sat us at a table just big enough for two people. It was eye level of the back stage with just enough room for one girl to dance on a pole. Way too close! Our waitress, Ms. Chardonnay, came over to our table. "Welcome to Déjà Vu, where we satisfy your wettest, wildest dreams while you sit in your seat. What are you ladies having to drink?"

I looked at her; she looked at me and I didn't know what to think. "Okay," I decided, "We're playing hard tonight, so we might as well go all the way. Bring us some shots of Patron. Añejo. Four of those. Two for my friend, two for me."

I looked around at the girls."Do y'all allow touching in here, Ms. Chardonnay?"

"Just depends. If the money and tips are right, well…"

Then she walked away. Lord have mercy! This girl had an ass on her. Hell, she could have sat a glass of Chardonnay on it and walked around. Much different than back in the day. There was an Asian girl, two Mexicans, Black, White, and even a big German one. Oh, no. Three blacks. Or so I thought, until she passed by with her tray, seating some customers, and I heard her speak. She looked black, but she was speaking Spanish. Panamanian, maybe? Hell, I don't know. These days I can't tell who's who. All of these girls were fine. We didn't have it like that back in our day. You had a few fine ones that stood out and the rest were just okay.

The girls smoked blunts, black and black and gold. I brought my special pack of Fantasia cigarettes by Nat Sherman. I like to smoke sometime while I'm drinking. They go right with the occasion. I didn't see not one old person working in there. Gotta have some old dogs still around. I couldn't believe we were the only two left. They had girls dancing on the bar so, if you sit there, they were squatting right in your face. They had a rope that looked like a vine and every so often you saw a girl swing from one side to another on the rope.

"Hot damn. This shit is wild," I said, "This place sho' ain't for sissies. You better be ready to play hard if you come in here."

Chardonnay came with our drinks. Boy, was I ready for one. The margarita I had before we left the hotel had worn off. The damn shoes and boots that these girls were wearing made our tall shoes and boots back in the day look like flats. They had to be at least 6-8 inches, if not more. I saw belly piercing, nipple piercing, over the eye piercing, lip, and tongue piercing. And as the kids at my school say, "A lot of these girls were tatted."

When we were on stage, you maybe had two girls with small cute tattoos, like a butterfly on their back, a dragon on their shoulder, a heart on one of their breasts. Tattoos have been taken to another whole level! And the most piercing was to have about five holes in one ear and maybe, just maybe, every now and then you would see someone with a small diamond stud in their nose. Now, I must say, some of them looked damn good! Like one of the Hispanic girls, she had her navel pierced and the same matching earring on her nipples. The German girl with blonde hair had a tattoo like an anklet around her ankle; it was nice. No. I forgot the kids at school say, "banging" or "hot." We finished our first round of drinks.

We were drinking Patron, and talking shit. Melissa started talking about how we used to be some bad bitches back in our day.

I said, "Yes, we were girl, but now we're way too old for this shit. How did we ever manage to work all night and make it to class the next day?"

"I don't know, but we made it. I wouldn't be able to move for a week if I tried to do this shit and get up and go to school the next day."

"Well, what do you think?" I asked.

"We were young then. How old were you when you started dancing, Valerie?"

"I was eighteen years old."

"And I was nineteen. How old do you think these girls are? What do you think the age group is around here? Looks like the oldest one in here is our waitress, Chardonnay, and she's probably no older than twenty-five or six."

"Look at the Asian girl when she goes up on stage again. I bet she ain't no more than twenty-one," I said.

"She looks twelve."

"You know they hafta be at least twenty-one now so they can serve drinks," I said.

"Thin and limber as a fish. Did you see what she just did with her legs?"

"Baby," I said, "we can't do that kinda shit no more."

"Oh, come on, Valerie. You're not that much bigger than you were back then. What were you then, about ninety-five pounds? Now you're a hundred and ten."

"Stop, girl! I'm a buck fifteen! If I could just get rid of my stomach pouch and some of this cellulite on the sides of my thighs, I might be fine again. I'd hafta get a nip-tuck, though. No, make that a complete makeover."

"Well, is that all? That's nothing," Melissa said, "I need to get my boobs replaced. I've had these since the dancing days. You remember my regular customer named Charlie? He paid for them. He was a good one. He helped me out a lot throughout college. My butt keeps getting bigger and bigger, but it's flat as hell."

"These white girls now got butts like a sista."

"Hell, there weren't any white girls with big butts back in our day, and you know it," Melissa said. "So if I ever win the lottery, that's just one of the things I'm getting fixed! I've got a bad knee, varicose veins, bunions, a whole laundry list."

"Melissa, you still crazy! I remember that show you used to put on where you had the swords with the fire, and you'd be greased down in baby oil and doing the back bend and all that kinda shit. Can you still do any of that?" I asked her.

"Hell, no, but right about now, this Patron is making me feel like maybe I could. We need to show these youngsters how it's supposed to go! How we used to do it."

"I know that's right! Waitress, bring us another round," I said.

"Okay, I'll be right back. You ladies are getting tight!"

Melissa grinned at her. "You got that right."

Chardonnay came back with the drinks. "This round is on the house. Compliments from the manager and bartender. Oh yeah…he sent a message, too. He wants to know if he could join the two of you.

I said, "Oh, damn! Tell him to come on down!"

That Chardonnay, she was a bad girl. There was no way a man could come in here and not give her ass a tip. She was sexy, pretty, and that outfit she had on was dope. I could tell those boots she had on cost a pretty penny too. They played this song called "Five Star Chick," and I was listening to the words and I was saying, "Hey, Ho. I like that shit! That sounds like me."

The next thing I knew, two men were coming to our table. It was pretty dark in there, so I could hardly see their faces, and when they came up to sit down, they introduced themselves. One was Dennis, the manager, and the other was I think he said Hal? They sat down and we all started talking. I introduced us. "This is my friend Melissa, and I'm Valerie."

Dennis was the manager." So what brings you ladies out to Déjà Vu tonight?"

Before I could say another word, Melissa was over there, shaking and grinding, and, I think, a little bit tipsy from her third shot of Patron. She said," My friend and I came to check out the place and maybe even dance. We are two old retired dancers, and we used to be some bad girls back in our day."

"Well now, you know we can make that happen. I knew there was something about you two. First, I thought you guys were undercover. Then I said, no, they're having way too much fun. I saw you guys giving out tips to the girls once they came to the back stage."

"Yeah, I remember what it was like to be up there ass-buck-naked and no one clap or give you a tip! I still remember some of those bad nights!" I said.

"Well, ladies, I want you to enjoy yourselves and when you're ready let me know, and I will have Chardonnay take you back to the dressing room so you can get up on stage once more for old times sake."

Melissa said, "What! Never! I don't think I could."

But I was grinning and said, "I'll be ready in a minute! Now what was your name again?"

"Dennis," he said.

"You know you look so, so familiar. Dennis? Have you ever been to or worked in a club in another part of Tennessee?"

"Matter of fact I have. I use to work as a bartender when I was younger at this club called The Mermaid, out near the Naval Base."

"Damn! That is you. Don't you remember me? You use to give me a ride home. I used to hold your little girl in my lap when we picked her up from the baby sitter after work, until we got to my apartment. Until one night you wanted me to spend some time with you and not go home to that crazy nut I was living with? Remember now. Is it coming back to you? Look, you had to be about twenty-five years old. I was twenty-one. Anyway, ain't this a small world? My nickname was Spider. You still got a bald head. Grey mustache now, but you know I never forget a bald head, especially when it looks as good as yours," I said.

He blushed. "Spider, Spider, I can't believe it's you."

"Dennis, you've aged gracefully, and that head still looks just as good as it did back then. You still look good, Dennis. I remember like it was yesterday. You said, 'Spend the night with me. Let's stop and have some breakfast and coffee. ' I told you, 'No, I hafta get home. ' I didn't want to tell you that I really, really wanted to, but was afraid to tell you that I was living with a monster who would kill me if I came home late. Thank God, I grew up and got away from that nightmare. So, what? You own this fine establishment now?"

"Yeah, I saved enough money bartending to open up my own club. That little girl who you used to hold is now a married young lady. She moved to Washington, D. C., and has a job working for the U. S. Patent Office. Plus, her mother lives in Philadelphia and she likes to be near and keep up with her. She never got custody of her from me, but now that her daughter is grown, she has finally cleaned up her act and is living a clean and sober life.

"Well, well. I don't believe this. Who is your partner that my friend Melissa is talking to?"

"Oh, that's my son. He will be taking over one day, so, right now, he's my right arm man. I don't know what I'd do without him."

"How old is he, twenty-one?"

"No, he's thirty."

"Better be careful. Melissa might try to rape him."

"Oh! He's a big boy and she's a big girl, they'll be okay. Come on Spider, I mean Val. Okay, if I call you Val? You got to let me show you around."

The place was huge. They had a kitchen with a chef named Morgan and a quiet room, where the dancers could rest up and relax a bit. The dressing room was fabulous. Nothing like back in my day when you had small lockers, the dressing counter and toilet and sink all together. Everything was put together very well. He had a fully furnished office upstairs. He introduced me to a few of the dancers and they all addressed me as Ms. Valerie.

I thought, "Damn, I must look old. They keep calling me Ms. Valerie." I hate when they Ms. me, or Ma'am me, ugh!

"Okay, now that you've seen the place, come on! Let's get the party started. One of my dancers, Amber, is about your size. She'll help you find something to put on. I'm leaving. I'll see you out front. I'm going to check on Melissa and my boy. Don't want her hurting him before the night is over."

"Oh, damn," I thought, "I've had too much Patron, and where the hell, what the hell, how the hell? This is crazy."

The next thing I knew, I was changed into a damn uniform and it was something else. Didn't mention to Melissa that I had gotten an augmentation as a college graduation present to myself. Couldn't afford it when I was dancing and hustling to pay for my college degree. "Okay," I thought, "Valerie, let's suck it up. Oh! I can't do this shit. What was I thinking! Too late now."

Then I saw Amber looking at me. "Ms. Valerie, may I ask, how old are you?"

"Baby, I'm fifty-five."

"Damn, I hope I can still look like that at fifty-five. Your body is still tight!"

"I'm old though, girl. I got miles on this body."

"I can't tell."

"Thanks, you make an old girl feel good," I said.

Then I started thinking, "Oh! My Patron is wearing off and I'm coming to my senses. How am I gonna get out there now?"

Then I heard the D. J. saying, "We have a special treat for you tonight. We have Ms. Spider. She's a blast from the past. She's here having a little fun tonight and to show some of these Divas how the big girls use ta do it! Let's bring her on: The sexy Ms. Spider."

I told Amber, "No, you go. I can't do it."

"Yes, you can, Ms. Val. You look hot. Go." She paused for a moment. "Okay, Ms. Val, wait. Here, take two pulls off of this."

I took a pull of that stuff she rolled and I was gone! The DJ was saying, "Come on out, Ms. Spider. We're waiting for you. We want to see how a black widow spider spins her web."

He put a slow song on, something I could keep up with. It was one of my favorite R. Kelly songs, called *Wine for You.* I can't tell you what I did or how I looked to all of those men out there, but it must have been okay, 'cause they were whistling, hollering, shouting and throwing money. I couldn't hardly see shit without my glasses, but I looked down and I saw several twenty-dollar bills, and Dennis came up and placed a one hundred-dollar bill on the side of my g-string. Oh damn, just like back in the day.

Now, let me describe that outfit I got from Ms. Amber. It was a blue-green, covered in sequins, all one piece that snapped up around my neck. Thank goodness, that helped hide that little hump in the middle of my stomach. The top was shaped like a star, so my breasts showed through the openings of the star. Perfect fit. What a rush; it felt like old times. Melissa even came up and put a twenty on the stage. She was so fucked up. We had lost our ever-loving minds! I finished my song and ran off the stage. Amber was back there waiting for me and she said, "Ms. Val, you're a G!"

"Okay, whatever that means."

"How did you do that thing with your arms where you reached around and touched your boobs?"

I said, "That's old school, girl. You don't know nothing about that?"

She shook her head and grinned, "It's a good thang."

She gave me a high five. I got dressed and asked her, "Can I have another puff of that stuff?"

She lit up, took a long pull herself, and passed it to me. I puffed, and just as I finished, Dennis showed up. He said, "Girl, you still got it. You can dance for me anywhere, anytime, any day. Say, how did you get that cigarette to hold on your nipples the whole time you were dancing?"

"What time is it? We have got to get the hell out of here!"

"It's two already. Stay with me until closing and we will take the two of you back to your hotel. Where are you guys staying?"

I told him Opryland Hotel, and he said, "Please stay, Val, and for the last time, Spider, will you please have breakfast with me?"

I smiled. "Yes, I will."

JESSICA

A dozen years ago I moved back to dull old Memphis, where I swore I'd never return. Oh, I hated to leave Los Angeles, where the weather was always great most of the time, always something to do, somewhere to go, and someone new to meet. I always had fun. What a wonderful feeling waking up to a view of palm trees swaying and snow on the mountains and the crashing of waves to sleep by at night. Living with windows open every day and enjoying the nice breeze. I knew I would miss going to the Long Beach Jazz Festival, or taking a day trip to Glen Ivy for ultimate relaxation. I loved going to Big Bear in the fall, leaving with shorts and putting my fleece jacket on once I arrived. Driving up to where the air was fresh, clear, and clean, covered with snow in the winter. I would miss riding Amtrak for the day to San Diego. I'd miss the Rose Bowl Parade, and Moon Shadows restaurant on a full moon night.

But I knew it was time to go home. I was single, with two kids, and parents getting old and sick who needed me. And it was time for my children to see and get to know their grandparents.

Moving back to Tennessee was the hardest decision I ever made, but that decision ultimately led me to the only man I have ever loved, and to a life filled with secrets.

I asked my brother to find me a realtor in town. We needed help finding a nice place to live. Not too close, but not too far from Mom and Dad or the rest of the family. I settled for Midtown. It kind of gave me that feeling of Los Angeles and South Pasadena all in one. People riding bikes, walking their animals, skating, hanging out at Starbucks, and walking to the neighborhood bars. I see people driving around in all the latest models of cars, biracial couples, and kids, too. Yeah, this was my part of town, reminds me so much of L.A.

I didn't have time to come here first and do my homework on the house myself, so I trusted the realtor. My brother hooked me up with him so I felt he was safe. He found me a five bedroom, two-story, three and a half bath on Pecan Grove Lane; it was beautiful. I never could have gotten a house like this at this price anywhere in Los Angeles County! So I went for it. All transactions were done by phone, fax, and computer. The realtor sent pictures of the house by email. He also informed me of the schools close by for the kids and everything. We arrived in August. My brother took care of obtaining the right movers in Los Angeles and everything arrived on time as planned. All of our furniture was intact, no mishaps. Everything fit perfectly in this house. Seemed as if it was just made for us.

All my family members seemed happy to have me and the kids back home. It took a couple of months to get everything in order, get the kids adjusted in school, and get my bearings back. A lot had changed, yet a lot was still the same. We settled in and started several routines. One was spending Sundays with Mom and Dad. We always met them at church and afterwards had dinner with them. After about six months of being with them every Sunday, I noticed that Dad was starting to have a bit of a memory loss. When I mentioned it, however, he denied it.

The next thing I knew, he went and bought himself a new Cadillac with the GPS and OnStar System that would get him home if he got lost. My poor mom was at his mercy. She never learned how to drive.

One night around midnight, I received a call from some strange young lady asking if I was the daughter of Mr. Jay and Sally Banks. She said, "Well, they are here in Rossville and seem a bit lost. Mr. Jay told me he was going home but Ms. Sally said they didn't live in Rossville. She asked me to call you."

"Thanks, I appreciate your call. Can you please hold them there until I can get someone to meet them? I will send one of my cousins who live in Rossville to pick them up. Shouldn't take her more than 20 minutes."

Thank God, they were at least where I knew someone. It would take me about an hour to get there. I called Effie. She's the youngest and I was sure she could go get them. I prayed she was home or awake."Effie, hi. I hate to bother you so late, but it's an emergency. My mom and dad are lost out near you. Do you think you could get them back on track and head them in the right direction home?"

"Sure, girl. I think Uncle Jay is getting like my daddy, God bless his soul. I have to come to town in the morning so I think I'll just follow them home and bring my things with me. I'll stay till morning and that way I will know they'll get home safe."

"Thanks, girl. Call me when y'all get home so I can rest my mind at ease. You know I'm going to have to stop that old man from driving. It's too dangerous out here these days," I said.

"I know that's right."

Effie called me at one fifteen, just as I was dosing off. "When we got to the house, Uncle Jay was sitting in the car for a long time asking your momma, 'Whose house is this? We need to get home to our own house. ' It took both of us to convince him this was his house and he finally got out."

I lay there and thought, "I have got to do something about this. I think my dad is slipping into dementia."

The next day, I started looking at nursing homes for the two of them. I knew I would have to fight with my other siblings but everyone else had husbands, grown kids and grandkids, and always seemed so busy. I was the only single one and the only one with young kids. I thought, "For now, I'm gonna give it some time."

Six months later, my dad's situation was getting worse. My sisters and brothers just thought it was cute and a normal part of old age. Me, on the other hand, I was worried to death. They had no idea of the things he had done around the house and just how far gone he was. They weren't there when he urinated in the flowerpot at the grocery store, or blurted out in church to Pastor Clarke," Shut the fuck up so we can get the hell out of here."

Everyone meets at the house for Thanksgiving, so I decided that was the best time to talk with them, after dinner once everyone settled down. I brought all the pamphlets and brochures that I had collected, hoping we could all come to some kind of agreement. I had brochures from Kirby Pines, Fox Bridge, Belmont Village, as well as prices for a live in caregiver. They're all expensive, but they always gave us the best of everything growing up so I want to do the same for them.

Everyone wanted some time to look over the information that I'd given them. So we set a time to meet again on the following Sunday after church service, another place where we all came together for them. I explained that we needed to decide soon because our parents are drastically changing.

With that exception, things seemed to be going fine. The three of us were adjusting, and I'd accepted being back home. I had enough money left over after buying the house for us to live comfortably until I decided how or what I would like to do to maintain a lifestyle here in Tennessee.

Then, after that first year of living in our new house in Tennessee, problems started. The first problem was the kitchen sink. It started backing up water, and I noticed that the bathtub upstairs in the kids' bathroom drained really slowly. No biggie, I thought. This is an older house.

I called a plumber out to take a look at it and he informed me that the pipes in this house gotta be, hafta be, absolutely must be replaced. ASAP. They were very old and needed major work. He said, "Your problem is coming from that large pecan tree in the back yard. It has grown into your pipeline and I will have to dig and tear all of the pipes out and replace them. For a house this size it will cost about ten thousand to take care of it all."

I told him I would be in touch. I wanted to get a few more estimates as well as contact the real estate agent who sold me this damn house. And I thought to myself, "No wonder this street is called Pecan Grove Lane."

The next week while we were in bed, I heard a loud scratching noise. It sounded like someone was trying to break in. I'd heard it before earlier in the week. It was around the same time, ten p.m., but I had ignored it. I thought it was just me, or just the sound of the house settling and me getting use to it. Then I heard it again.

I panicked and ran to the phone to call my neighbor. I hated to call him so late, but he assured me when I first moved in that any time, any problem, I could just give him a call. When I explained to Mr. Bill what was going on he came right over. He had his flashlight and he went straight up to the attic. I could hear him walking around and then I heard him make a big stumble. I thought, "Oh God, all I need is a lawsuit from my neighbor."

I heard him say, "Get! Get!" and then, after a pause, "Oh, shit!"

He came down after what seemed like an eternity, although it was actually about ten minutes. "Guess what?" he said, "You've got a raccoon family living in your attic. You need to have a trap set. Call the wildlife center. They will send someone out to catch them."

The next morning, I found Lemon's Wildlife Service in the Yellow Pages. They advised me the fee to come out and set a trap would be two hundred fifty dollars. The agent who came out said I would know when the raccoons were trapped because I would hear a lot of noise. A week went by and nothing, then, about the third day into the second week, I heard it. There was a loud squealing noise and a whole lot of shaking. I called Lemon's, and the next morning they came out. It was just as Mr. Bill said, a family of raccoons. Momma and two babies. This house was becoming kind of scary. What could happen next?

MABEL

I had been working on my mom for several months, telling her we really need to trade in her Cadillac. It was three years old, and I didn't want to be driving around in some out-of-date used car that could stop on us at any time. And I am the one who does the driving, because Momma can't really get around the way she used to. I don't really mind. Momma takes good care of me and I take care of her, too.

She finally saw the light, so I went into the dealership she likes, and I saw what I wanted right away. I was looking inside, inhaling that new car smell, when the salesman came out on the lot.

"She's a beauty, isn't she? Let me get the keys for you, so you can try her out." He extended his hand. "My name's Joel Cavanaugh."

"Mabel Sutton."

"Well, Ms. Sutton, let's take this car out for a test drive, and I'll fix you right up."

The Cadillac drove like a dream. I fell right in love with it. I explained to Mr. Cavanaugh that I would be driving, but my mom would be purchasing the car.

He nodded, understanding completely. "Here's what we'll do. Now, you say your mom doesn't get around well, right? So why don't you take this new Cadillac home, drive her around in it for a few days, let her get the feel of it, and let me know if and how she likes it. I'll just need you to leave her old car and the keys and a copy of your driver's license with me. I'll have my guys check it out and we can go from there."

I told Mr. Cavanaugh, "I think I can handle that."

I left my... no, my mother's old Cadillac and took the new one. It was fully loaded, candy apple red, tinted windows, tan leather interior, navigation system with turn by turn OnStar system, XM satellite radio with hard drive set up to record all of your favorite music, all temperature seats in the front, lumbar programmable seating, Bluetooth compatible, chrome wheels. This car had the hardtop and drop top. Umh. Umh. Umh. Just call me little red! Not Mabel. And oh, I can't forget the keyless remote start-up. Brand, damn, spanking new! So, I left that old ass Cadillac. They don't even make them anymore. It was a piece of shit anyway, a lemon.

As I drove off, Mr. Cavanaugh was smiling and waving goodbye and probably saying to himself, "Got another one. Ain't no way she will be bringing that car back."

I left the dealership and headed down 41A Highway to Golf Club Lane, straight to my mom's house. When I pulled up to the gate that led to her circular driveway, she could see me coming, but I knew she didn't recognize me in this new car. I knew she'd love it. She's a Cadillac girl, always has been, always will. And, at her age, she ain't hardly changing. My momma could do a commercial for Cadillac. They would make so much money they wouldn't hafta overcharge people. One of Momma's sayings is, "If you ain't driving a Cadillac, you ain't in a real car. They are the next best thing to ride in besides an airplane."

Momma says, "You see that new Black President we got? What kinda car does he ride in? Cadillac. So, if the president rides in one, what that tell ya? He rides in the best."

She says, "Yo daddy always kept me riding in style with the latest model Cadillac every year. He's passed away now and I still hafta ride in a Cadillac, even if I hafta get it for myself. Lord knows he worked hard enough to see fit for me to live well, even though he's gone on home now."

I'm her driver, and I mean her driver! I drive her everywhere, to the store for one item, Nashville for lunch, Kentucky for the Kentucky Derby, Lambert's for dinner where they throw the rolls, up in Branson, Missouri, and to church every Sunday—where she teaches Sunday school.

I went in the house and I told her, "Here's the deal, Mom. The man at the dealership said to bring this new Cadillac home and keep it for the weekend. He said, 'Let your momma see how she likes it.' I'll ride you around wherever you need to go for a few days and if you like it, it's yours. Same low monthly payments, no money down, just a new car for you, and they will take your old car as a down payment. So go get dressed so we can take it for a spin."

At age eighty, she still looks good and still has a sound mind. She's always drinking her Pepsi and eating croissants. Maybe that's the key to her longevity. I should start drinking Pepsi and eating croissants.

She said, "I read in the paper about a new steak house that just opened up in Nashville called Flemings. Baby, I want to go there. We need to put that car on the highway to see if it's as good as they say."

"Okay, Momma, I'll wait for you to get dressed. I'm gonna go back there to my old room and watch TV while you get ready."

It took her about forty-five minutes to get ready. When she came out of her room, just patting on her little hair, she had on her red St. John knit pantsuit, tan leather flat shoes, and a necklace of rubies and diamonds, complete with matching bracelet and earrings. She also had her tan Coach purse and was totally matching the car. I helped her out the door, set the alarm for her, and off we went down 41A highway to interstate24 headed for Nashville.

Momma loved it. "Let's see how fast this thing can go, girl! Step on it!"

We got there in record time. The speed limit was seventy, but I was doing ninety and she didn't say a word. Didn't even flinch. She loved going fast, even though she couldn't drive a lick. My daddy was stationed overseas a lot, so I learned to drive early. She wanted to look in the mirror to make sure her make-up was just right and she kept looking for the switch to turn the light on. I told her, "Momma, now in this car, all you have to do is touch it and the light will come on.

She said, "Oh, Baby, I like this car."

Something about the mirror in Cadillac's that she just loved. By the time we got to Flemings, it was one p.m. Right on time for lunch. We had a great lunch. She treated, of course, and then she said, "Stop at that Cracker Barrel place on the way back. I just want to pick up some of that old-fashioned candy they sell like I used to get in the good old days when you were a little girl."

We went in and she picked what she wanted and we headed back. On the way back, she said, "Baby, I really like this one, especially how it seems to be warming my behind. Is it me or is there something in these seats?"

I smiled, "Yeah, Momma, it comes with heated seats."

"Lord, things sure have changed. I never thought I'd live to see something like this, but I'm glad. Tell that man we'll take it. Can you get him on the phone? This car got a phone in it too?"

"Yeah, Momma, but they're closed now. I'll call him Monday," I promised her.

"Hey, Mabel, stop me at Kroger so I can get some fresh greens for Ms. Eddie to cook for me on Monday."

My momma was something else. I dropped her off with her groceries and told her I would be back in the morning to pick her up for church.

She said, "Be here on time. You know I gotta teach my Sunday school class and I don't want to be late, especially not in my new car. Be here no later than 9:15."

"Yes ma'am, I'll be here on time.

I headed for my girlfriend Renee's house over on Dandelion Court, so I could show her my new ride. We could go over to Smooth Jazz Nights and have a glass of wine before I went home. There was always some eye candy in there to look at. I'm always shopping! Not buying anything, though. I called her from the car phone, and when she answered, I said, "Hey girl, come outside. I'm in your driveway.

"Mabel, girl, I almost didn't answer the phone 'cause I didn't recognize this number. You…ahhhhh…you're a bad bitch."

"Yeah! Yeah! Yeah! And you know it. This is my mom's new ride. You know I'm broke."

I can't tell !"

We had a great time at Smooth Jazz Night. We each had two glasses of wine. Then, I took her home. I was driving down the road, looking fine, and looking forward to the last Friday of the month, so I could show my new car off to all my girls at the book club.

I got momma to church on time and I even stayed with her this time. I was there for Sunday school and morning service. I wasn't gonna do anything wrong to mess up my chances of being able to drive her around in her beautiful new car. After church we had dinner in the fellowship hall.

I went home with her and we did our usual Sunday routine. We read the Sunday paper together, then watched T. D. Jakes at four p.m. After T. D. Jakes, that was usually her telephone time with her little church lady friends.

"Okay, Momma, I'm getting ready to go. I'm gonna run by and say hi to Lynn."

"Okay, Baby. Give Cousin Lynn a hug from her Auntie."

Then the phone rang. She answered, "Hello, oh, hey, Sister Dunlap. Just fine. Hold on one minute."

She had her hand over the mouthpiece of the phone and asked me, "What time do I need to be ready?"

"I'll be here by ten."

"Okay. I'll be ready, baby. Lock me in."

"First thing in the morning, I'll call Mr. Cavanaugh at the dealership."

EVA

The day came, and Pastor and his wife's anniversary celebration looked like it was going to turn out great. I pulled up into the parking lot, and it was full. Cars everywhere. There are so many people who love Pastor Clarke.

I knew I looked good. I found out they were wearing turquoise and brown and my outfit was the same. More important, I damn sure knew I looked better than that so-called First Lady, Sister Clarke. William and the kids were on their way, and would arrive soon. He had to take Evan Laire' to get something from the mall that she needed for school the next day. He's such a great dad. If my daughter only knew, she would hate me. And if my son Brandon knew, he would cry. I know it would break his heart. Sometimes I feel so bad. I know William can't help the way things turned out for him health wise, but the only way I've survived these last three years is because of Pastor-U-Know. Okay, girl, I told myself. Snap out of it. Get yourself together and go on inside, and save a seat for your family.

I walked in and as soon as I saw the two of them sitting there together, I felt sick to my stomach. I could feel my heart racing and I was getting a little warm. I thought, "Be cool and keep walking."

The usher was directing me to a seat on the right hand side of the sanctuary, same row and seat where I always sat. I felt as if it was reserved just for me and he could always see me from that seat. I looked over where they had specially decorated two seats for the pastor and his wife. The sign said, "In Honor of the Greatest Pastor & First Lady Clarke."

And, yes, he saw me. That made my heart skip a beat. This has gotten old now, and I know I will never leave William. I'm sure he will never leave Sister Clarke. So what do I do? How do I get out of this mess? I want out! Yet I love being in. Oh God, please help me! Then my hubby and kids walked over to the pew, and I moved down to make room for them.

They had a nice program lined up. This little bitty woman sang who could hardly talk, but when she started singing, she didn't even need a microphone. Her voice was powerful. She sang this song about your blessing being on the way. She had two young men with her; one played saxophone and the other guitar. They each had a solo part in the song. She introduced them as her nephews. What talented young men. Then, this older lady, Sister Ghoston, came up. I recognized her, because she always helps with the flower ministry. She read a poem about the pastor and his wife.

Then I started to drift off. Next on the program was the offering, then a selection from the choir, followed by Pastor and Wife gift presentation - first, the usher board, then, the deacons, the mother board, the youth choir…

It was nice, but I sat there in a daze, kept thinking that should be me sitting there next to him. I should be the one receiving all the praise along with him, but the facts remained. It wasn't me and never will be. I needed to let it go.

The guest pastor was introduced by Pastor Clarke's son, Ronnie. I hear he is so scandalous, but you know what they say, "Fruit don't fall too far from the tree."

The guest pastor was from Clarksville. He started out with a song and he sounded great. It was called, *You Won't Leave Here Like You Came (In Jesus' Name),* Then he asked everyone to turn to the book of Romans, chapter 12:1-21. Then chapters 13 and 14. It really hit home for me.

After he finished the message, he asked people to come up for prayer. He said, "If you are doing something that you know is wrong in the sight of God, if you've been carrying it around for a long time, if you just can't seem to break free, now is the time for your salvation. Come on up. Today is your day."

Before I knew it, the tears started running down my face, and I was headed up to the altar. He prayed for several people. Some were screaming, some started shouting and some fell out. I couldn't move. He came to me. "Sister, God has put it on my heart to tell you that today is your day. He's gonna remove that burden, that problem, that issue that you've been caring around for so long. Repeat these words after me, sister. Lord, I am sorry for everything I've done wrong. Please forgive me, take away any bad habits and wrongdoings I may have. Save me and make me whole. He's gonna release that thing from you right now! In the name of Jesus, you are set free."

Afterwards, I went back to my seat and my daughter Evan Laire' said, "Momma, are you okay?"

"Yes, Baby, momma is okay now."

Then the pastor came up and gave words of thanks. Sister Clarke came up and gave her words of thanks and announced there would be food served for all in the fellowship hall immediately after service. My husband and I and our kids all went to eat. The pastor and his wife were walking around hand in hand to each table thanking members and guests for coming and for the great gifts they had received. When he passed our table, I could hardly look at him, but for the first time I really saw him. He was a man, just like any other. A cheating, married, supposedly God-fearing man. A man who was supposed to stand for something, someone to be respected, someone with morals, but instead, he was just another man, who happened to be married. And I was a married woman who knew better." Never again," I thought, "This is where it ends."

It felt as if something had been lifted off me. And just like clockwork when everything was over, I got a text from him, "See you in one hour, you know where."

I replied, "NO, NOT NOW, NOT EVER AGAIN."

He texted back, "You know you can't resist me. You'll see; you'll be calling."

Quite a few Sundays have passed now, and so far the thrill is still gone. I no longer have those feelings that used to come up every time I saw him, and no more of those panicky feelings inside when I see him with his wife. No more sick to my stomach feelings when I lie to William that I've been over my sister's house. No more crying in the shower as I try to wash away his smell, his touch, the guilt when I lie in bed every night next to my husband. And poor Sister Clarke, I pray for her.

I've asked and I know God has forgiven me. I will never, never, ever, do what I've done again… At least not with the Pastor-U-know!

William and I and the children are still going to church. The kids and I go each and every Sunday, even when William can't make it due to his work schedule. The pastor has tried several times to get friendly with me through the kids, but I promised myself never, ever, again. I asked God to forgive me and I'm sticking to it.

SARA

Most evenings, once it gets cool, I go outside and work in my yard. I just love flowers, especially my azaleas and my rose bushes. I've won yard-of-the-month every summer for the past five years, ever since I left my job and took that severance package.

I get by with my social security, my savings, and being real careful with the severance money. I keep a close eye on those folks down at the bank. I don't trust those gangsters, and that's all they are, just a bunch of legal gangsters. Seems like they charge you for everything, to put money in, take money out, to check your balance, to look it up in the computer, to transfer. I know I've got enough to last me, but I've always been like that. I worry about money.

I'd like to have at least something left to leave to my daughters when I'm gone. I wouldn't want to be around to see it, though. I'm afraid they'd go crazy and go through my hard-earned money in no time. I know that Becky. She would have all hers spent in a matter of months, or maybe a matter of weeks! My big girl, she'd do better. She's a little more sensible about money. They really never have done without, the way I did. I grew up poor, and I promised myself, "When I get grown, I will never be broke again."

My daughters have been successful, though, made good lives for themselves. And they always think about me. Last Christmas they gave me an mp3 player loaded with all my favorite songs.

I was out working in my yard, thinking about all this and listening to my favorite oldies station, when I heard, "Go out and get your Powerball ticket today. It's a big one. Don't let your numbers win without you."

What? The Powerball was $281 million? I went into the house and got some dirt off my face and hands, then headed over to the convenience store to pick up a ticket. The line was long. Usually there is hardly anybody in there playing, but I guess for a chance to win $281 million for a dollar, folks are willing to wait a little bit

I decided to pick the same numbers I've always played. 'They'll either work or they won't,' I thought. 'Let's see, my birthday is 6/11, my oldest daughter's is 7/18, and my baby daughter's is 12/10.'I always use a combination of those. Then I drove over to the plant nursery. I had $500 I'd recently won at the casino, and it was burning a hole in my pocket. I used part of it on some new heritage roses they had just gotten in from their supplier.

That Sunday was pastor and his wife's anniversary, and they asked me to do a reading. Then we had a guest pastor from Clarksville. He had a wonderful reputation, and I didn't want to miss that He gave a powerful message, about renouncing the past and moving forward in the light of the Lord.

There's this nice little family in the church. They always seem so happy, and I usually see them all together. When the visiting pastor did altar call and said, "Someone here has been doing something or has something on their heart that needs to change. Come on up and let me pray for you today, right now, that young mother went up by herself. The pastor said, "Today is your day. Repeat these words after me, sister. Lord, I am sorry for everything I've done wrong. Please forgive me, take away any bad habits and wrongdoings I may have. Save me and make me whole.' "

She was just crying and sobbing so loud. I thought to myself, "Hmm, she must have been really, really doing something terrible. Now what was her name again? Lorraine? No, that's her sister's name, the church secretary. Let's see. Oh, yes. Eva Halston. Her husband's name is William."

The pastor prayed for her and I know a whole lot more of them in here should've went up for prayer, too, but didn't. Anyway, I'm just gonna try to save my own soul and let everybody else worry about theirs.

After service, I stopped by the cupboard restaurant and got my usual for dinner, chicken and dressing. I just love their food, and I'm so glad that if I don't feel like it, I don't hafta cook. Long gone are those days for me.

There is a Mapco gas station close by the church. I stopped by there and picked up a copy of the Powerball winning numbers. When I finally got home I got out of my church clothes and took my ticket out of the nightstand. I sat down to relax and check the numbers. Of course, I couldn't find my reading glasses. I am getting so old, I can't see a damn thing without them.

Let's see—6, 7, 10, 11, 12, and the Powerball number, 18. Um, I had all of those. I had all of those numbers. About time, I never get the right numbers. Wait. What? What!? Oh my God. I got it right! Oh my God! All six of them! That's… I looked at the ticket again... oh my... $281 million dollars. Whew... Oh, I was hot. I was having a hot flash. Where was my fan? Where was the remote for the fan? Oh! I was sure I was gonna faint. Who should I call? No, no wait, I needed to think about this. Yes, call my daughters. No, call my sister. No. Yes. No. Yes. Oh, no. I was sweating bullets.

"Calm down, Sara," I told myself. "Take a deep breath. Do not tell a soul yet. My God, how will I keep this one under my hat? I will hafta come forward soon. Let's see. Let me look on the back of this ticket and sign it, too. Okay. Now I've signed it. Sara Ghoston.

"I will hafta show up in Nashville if I don't go back to the Mapco station where I bought this ticket. Um, guess I'll get ready to drive to Nashville 'cause ain't no way I'm going back over to Mapco. I'll go to Nashville tomorrow. No, let's see. I have 180 days to claim this money.

"Whew! Another hot flash. Gotta settle down, so I can think this out clearly. I think for now I just need to lie down for a while. Now, let's see, I need to put my ticket in a safe place. Hum... I know, I will put it…in my Raisin Bran cereal box. No one will find it there."

My goodness. I did not want everybody knowing my business. What was I going to do? I woke up, looking for my glasses so I could see the clock. It was three a.m. Damn, I must have passed out after that last hot flash, and the shock of winning. Lord Jesus. I just could not believe it was me. But here I was, awake and looking at a very valuable box of Raisin Bran.

My granny used to say, "Sometimes if you sleep on it, the answer will come to you, what decision you need to make. It'll be the first thing on your mind when you wake up." Granny was right, because now I had a clear feeling about what to do.

I decided not to claim my winning lottery ticket until the 179th day. I knew they give you 180 days. I decided to take out my calendar and start counting from today. Let's see, it was June 6th, and 179 days from then would be, umm, let's see. Okay, that would be December 5th, and maybe, just maybe, by then I would know if and who to tell.

VALERIE

When I went back to our table Melissa was grinning and all up on that young boy. She said, "I think I want to baby sit him."

He grinned at me, "I told her I need a momma to keep me warm for the night."

I said, "Oh, damn," before turning to Melissa and telling her privately, "We are gonna stay until closing and they will take us back to our hotel."

She was all smiles. Then I told her, "Girl, why did you let me get up there and make a fool of myself?"

"Hey, you were great! You looked awesome. Bitch, where's the money?"

We cracked up laughing and I said, "Let's count it."

I had a total of $300. I told her, "I'll give you half and we can use it to tip the girls working this last hour. That's the least we can do since I jumped in on their working time for fun." So from two until three a.m. we laughed, talked, drank, and passed out good tips.

"I am so glad I'm staying until Sunday evening," I thought. "There is no way I would be able to move Sunday morning. Wait, it's already Sunday!"

Dennis had a pretty nice club. Everyone seemed to take their job seriously. Security stayed until we left, and Dennis drove a nice Rolls Royce. I got in the front seat with him. His son and Melissa got in back. He had this nice jazz playing and I had a flashback. I remembered he always played Grover Washington when we were riding home from the club back in the day. He liked jazz and everyone that knows me know that I love jazz.

We went to the Waffle House for breakfast. They're open 24-7. Melissa and Al, as I found out since I finally got to get a word in and ask his name, were enjoying themselves. Melissa was all over him. He had a long ponytail and I knew she was crazy about a man with a ponytail and a six-pack to go with it. Oh! I hope she don't hurt the boy. I could see it in her eyes. She wasn't trying to eat no food; she was ready to go. I told her, "If we don't eat now we'll really pay later on this morning."

She had coffee, black, and two bagels with cream cheese. I had the works. I had the munchies from that stuff I smoked with that little girl Amber. I asked Dennis, "You're only having coffee?"

He said, "Yes, I plan on eating something else a little later."

I shivered! We ate and talked and went down memory lane. Talked about all the crazy dancers that we used to work with. Talked about all the different horror stories and hilarious ones as well. Then he got close to me and whispered in my ear. He said, "Val, Spider, Baby, let me do for you what I wanted to the last time I asked you out for breakfast, what? thirty years ago. I had a thing for you for such a long time and you never even noticed me. I always wanted to tell you more about how I wanted to be with you, but you just never ever noticed. So I held it in as long as I could until that night I had to ask and you turned me down flat. I would have taken you in to live with me and my daughter, but you just didn't seem to have a clue. Let me show you what you missed."

I thought to myself, "I never knew he was that sprung on me. What can he do? I've never been with a white boy. I've heard stories but never had the desire to try. I had plenty of chances back in the day. But back then, I was so hooked on that sorry ass man I was with. I couldn't see the forest for the trees, as they say. Well at fifty-five, what's to lose?

So I said, "Yes, Dennis, come with me. Let's go see what you and I have missed."

He asked the waitress for the check. I looked at my watch and it was five-thirty a.m. Melissa and I looked at each other and the four of us left walking side by side. We reached our rooms, and Melissa waved, "See you later girl. Call me."

She went her way and I went mine. As soon as I put the key card in the door and went in, he followed. All I could do was get into the room and sit on the sofa. I turned on my iPod and from there he went to work. Telling me that I smelled so good, and that I still had the same scent that he remembered so well. He pulled my shoes off first. Then he started kissing me, first on my neck, then my ears, then my breast. Then he said, "Excuse me, where is your bathroom?"

I pointed that way. He left the room. He had a little gut on him but not bad. He also had a small tattoo on his neck. It was a mouth with a tongue hanging out. He smelled good and his hands were so damn soft. He called out, "Valerie, could you come in here? I need you to help me with something."

When I stood up, I felt it. I had been drinking way, way too much. When I got in there, he'd found the hazelnut soy candles that I left around the tub from my previous night of relaxation and had lit them all. He had the water running and he held out his hand. "Join me."

He turned around, as he was on his knees whisking the water with his hand, making the almond oil bath gel bubble up all over the tub. He placed his hands on my hips and unzipped my skirt. It fell down to my knees. Then he pulled down my underwear, and said, "Just as I pictured."

Then he reached up and, from behind my back, he unhooked my bra. It fell to the floor. He started kissing me. From toe to head instead of head to toe. He had this beautiful dark brown hair all over his chest, mixed with a few grey strands in it also. What a sight, and he was so, so smooth. I could hear Will Downing singing *Pleasures of The Night*, and, oh, he was all over me. I thought, "Damn. You mean this is what I missed? I would have been all over him if I knew this was all in store for me. Young fool in love is what I was, back then. But damn that! Let's just enjoy now."

When he got through kissing and rubbing and licking me everywhere, I felt like a piece of Jell-O. Then he helped me in the tub and got in too. He just held me and then massaged me everywhere. I don't know how long we stayed in that water. Then we got out and he carried me to bed and I didn't need anything else. I was ready to just about lose my mind. He passionately kissed my lips, my eyelids, ears, breasts, my, my, everything. I was lost in passion. Then he got on top of me and went in and, oh! I've never been handled so, so, preciously. We went from him on top, to me on top, to me on the side, to him on the side, to me on my stomach until we finally, finally, reached the top of the hill! And he breathed into my ear, "See what we missed."

As I was falling asleep in his arms, my last thought was of Melissa. "Wonder what she's doing?"

When I woke up it was one p.m. and I had a huge headache. He was already up with the *USA Today* paper. I could smell the hazelnut coffee he'd made." Good morning, Spider. I mean, Val. I mean, good afternoon."

I looked around the room to see where in the fuck was I and what had I done. He said, "How do you like your coffee? Black or with cream?"

I said, "Cream and four sugars."

Dennis said, "I like mine black and sweet. Just like you."

I smiled, got out of bed and went to the bathroom. There I saw all of my clothes lying on the floor, candles burnt down to the ends. I brushed my hair, splashed water on my face, and grabbed the terrycloth robe that the hotel provided off the bathroom door. I called the front desk to arrange for a late checkout, then came back and sat next to him.

He put my cup of coffee on the table next to me, and took my hand. "I really enjoyed you last night at the club and this morning. Do you think we might be able to do it again?"

I said, "I don't live here. I was just here for work. I only come here once a year." I told him I was a principle at a school in another part of Tennessee. He couldn't believe it.

"Do you think I could come to visit you sometime and we could get to know each other a little better?" I smiled but avoided answering him directly. We made small talk and he said, "Call me any time, Val."

Then he called his son on his cell phone. They chatted and said they would meet at the car. We exchanged numbers and promised to keep in touch. As soon as I closed that door, I was running to the phone to call Melissa. I wanted to know what happened. She answered hello in this sexy voice and I said, "Girl…what happened?"

"It feels like Christmas. Santa brought me the main thing I had on my wish list early! That boy took me around the world like I've never been before. What about you?"

All I could say was, "It was heavenly."

"Val, you made this trip totally worthwhile. Last night was an amazing night, and I will never, ever forget it. So when are you leaving?"

"I'm driving home this afternoon late; how about you?"

"I'm leaving tonight."

"Girl, let's keep in touch. Where you live isn't but a three-hour drive for me."

"I know. Well, we've got each other's info and, if nothing more, I'll see you the same time next year."

I stretched and had another cup of coffee, then I checked out and made a quick run out to the mall. As I headed towards Interstate 40, I smiled as I reminisced. What a trip. I couldn't believe after all of these years, I ran into Diamond; never knew her real name was Melissa. And to see Dennis after all of these years, what a trip! I can't wait to tell my book club girls about my adventure. Can't wait to tell them their girl brought home a trophy for Principal of the Year. Last Friday of the month can't come fast enough. I'll be the first one at the book club meeting.

JESSICA

Two months more passed with no new problems. Knock on wood. Then one night, about a month later, I heard the kids screaming, "Momma! Momma, there are little bugs all over our wall and on the floor in our room."

It was termites in their bedroom and in the guest bedroom. Something told me to check the basement, and they were everywhere in there as well. My God, this house was infested. I knew, then and there, this house had major, major problems. I'd been sold a bad deal and someone was going to hafta answer for this. Someone was gonna hafta pay for all of this shit, and it wasn't gonna be me. None of these problems had been mentioned when I bought this house.

That's how I found him. I called around and asked around to see if anyone knew a good lawyer. My sister said, "Ask Cousin James. He may know someone. He no longer practices law. He got disbarred in 1999 for… Well, we won't go into that."

"Hmm," I thought, "I'd better leave that alone. Got enough problems. I'll just find someone myself." I looked the old fashioned way; I sat down at my computer and did a search. My computer was beginning to feel like my best friend. I just scrolled down and picked someone. That's how I found Mr. H. C. Charles.

I called and scheduled an appointment for Monday and of course, there was a consulting fee. Ugh, more damn money, but I needed someone and someone quick! His office was located in a small complex of office buildings off the main street downtown. His secretary greeted me.
"Make yourself comfortable and he'll be with you in just a second."

I waited thirty minutes past my scheduled appointment time, and I was beginning to get a little frustrated. Then out he came and my, oh, my. He was so handsome. He had that dimple thing going on in his chin and he had beautiful wavy salt and pepper hair. Too fine to be a lawyer in Tennessee. He had on a Rolex watch, looked to be about 6'3,"pretty white teeth, nice Armani suit, monogrammed initials on his cuff-linked shirt, and he smelled good. I quickly looked to see if he had a wedding band on his finger, and, he did.

Um, um, um, he moved me. Never met a white guy that moved me like him, but I was there for business. He said he would and could represent me. I thanked him, paid my retainer fee, and left. I thought, "Is it worth it? Should I just let it go? You're spending more money; this shit is adding up more and more." But I couldn't let it go. The past owner and realtor knew there were major problems with my damned house, but sold it to me anyway just the way it was. How could people be so mean? I trusted them. They really seemed like nice honorable people. It's hard to find people to trust these days.

Mr. Charles advised me that he would be contacting me soon and that he'd get started right away. I also took a few of his business cards when I left. Three days later he called. He sounded sooooo sexy on the phone. Deep voice, spoke well, didn't have that deep, deep southern drawl either. Um... um... um! Now I knew he was married, but my head was saying, "I know you're married, but are you happy?"

That's the line that me and my girlfriends back in L. A. used to say when we saw a fine ass married man. He started talking and I just listened. I tell you, it's a small world. Turns out the person who sold me the house is the client of a friend of his. Seems as if my realtor had been in trouble for doing the same thing to a couple in Arlington, and he was being sued by them as well. I also found out he had been in rehab twice. His father is a judge, mother is president of the Tennessee Bar Association, yet he's always been in some kind of trouble. He's known for doing all kinds of scandalous shit.

Attorney Charles said, "Before what he's done gets out and someone finds out about him messing up one more time, his people want to clear up the matter and try to agree to some type of settlement. Otherwise, he could lose his real estate license. They offered a settlement amount of $250, 000. If you decide to accept their offer, let me know and I will draw up the necessary paperwork. If so, we can get this resolved within the next two to three weeks. Sleep on it. Get out all of your receipts from all the repairs that you've paid. Then, when you are comfortable with what you want to do, let me know. Remember, you do have a right to file it in Circuit Court and perhaps take it to trial."

I agreed and the following week Attorney Charles settled the case. I had my people come and fix everything and, since the settlement was so generous, I went ahead and added a screened-in patio with pool and Jacuzzi. That whole process took about three months. One month later, my attorney called to see how I was doing and if the house was okay. I informed him that everything was fine and that we were finally really enjoying the house.

There was a lull in the conversation, then he asked, "Are you available to have lunch or dinner with me next week?"

"Yes, but I'm really a basic boring eater, a steak and potato girl," I warned him.

"I know exactly where to take you."

That's how it all started. I fell for him right away. He took me for dinner instead of lunch, and we ate at a beautiful steakhouse. The food was great, and he was too good to be true. He had it all together, what I call *a ladies' man*. He was good at everything he did.

After we'd been seeing each other for about six months, I gave him a key to my house. He was the first man that I ever gave a key to any place I've ever lived in my life. Not even my children's father from L. A. But this one, he deserved keys. He didn't want or ask for them, but I insisted.

We went to Jackson once a week for lunch for his business. Quiet dinners by candlelight. I still smell his cigars. Each and every Thursday for the next ten years.

We laughed and cried together. He was there for me when my parents finally moved into the retirement home, and he provided a shoulder when my dad died. He took care of me after my hysterectomy, and he supported me when I lost my big brother, and my best friend to cancer. He helped my family members whenever they needed him. I remember he got my niece out of trouble for getting in a fight at the casino. Some lady swore my niece stole her money, and security stepped in and it got ugly. He took care of it, and made it go away.

He gave me the most precious gifts a girl could ever want, like my breast augmentation for Valentine's Day, monthly visits to Eden Spa to get whatever I wanted, Botox, B12 shots, chemical peels, facials and massages, gift cards from King Furs, diamonds, and pearls. He even paid for my new car lease every four years. Let's see, the first four years I had a Mercedes, then the Porsche for two—that 911 was too fast for me—and the last four I settled for two cars, the Cadillac CTS and the Jaguar. Couldn't decide which one fit me best, so he got them both. He gave me jewelry from Tiffany's.

The whole family knew we were friends, but just how close of friends we really were, no one knew. The only people that regularly saw us together were the kids.

I can tell they miss H.C., too. Once they got used to him being around, they loved him. He was always there for them. We don't talk about it. He was like the father they never had.

He taught them how to ride a bike and build a tent. He got them their first skates and their first pet, a cute Yorkshire Terrier named Lucky. Took them to their first WWE wrestling match and art shows. He even taught them both how to drive. He showed up at all of their school plays, and gave them money for great report cards. He took them to basketball games, took them fishing, and hooked up and taught them how to use an electric drill and everything. Oh, they got so many gifts from him—Xbox 360, Wii, Laptops, iPods, and Nintendo DS. He showed them how to download music, bought them iPhones, colored contact lenses, visa gift cards, and their first real gold and diamond jewelry. He helped pay for so many of their wants, as well as needs. I really, really, miss him.

They asked, "What happened to H.C. momma? We don't see him anymore. He was so nice and good for you too, momma."

So what do I say? Some things are just best left being a secret?

H.C. often stayed late after the kids went to bed. He was always careful being around them when they had other friends over. He was pretty secretive, too. I found out that he'd never messed around on his wife before me. His wife was chosen for him by his parents. He was required to marry a nice Jewish girl and he did. She came from money. His father did the same with his mother. He married her for money as well. It was all planned. She came from old money, that slave-making money. She was a Branch/Loeb. Whatever she wanted, she got, and that's how she got his dad. Right away she wanted a son, and that's what she got.

I did a little researching for myself on him and found out that my mother used to cook for his parents and his grandparents. Now that's a small world. They lived over in this area called Chickasaw Gardens. I remember when I was a little girl, she would catch the bus and I would be watching the clock so I could run and meet that bus with my mother on it. She use to say, "Jessie, when I come back, I'm gonna bring you a whole lot of money."

That whole lot of money was one quarter back then. When I was a kid, a quarter was a whole lot of money!

I never told him that my mother worked for his grandparents. But he also never told me much about his family history either. I never saw it coming.

He seemed fine. I never knew he was sick. I knew he had a penile implant which made him pretty well-endowed. But I never knew he had colon cancer. Never knew he was half black and half white. His father was black. Big damn secret. No one ever knew, except his mother, of course, who his real father was. His dad, or, who he grew up to know and acknowledge as his dad, was white and didn't know either.

As I sat there at the funeral, I was thinking, there are so many people, and so many unknown faces here. I was looking and trying to match faces with all the stories he'd told me throughout the years. Like the cousin on steroids, and the friend who locked his wife in the house for a week and shaved her head bald when she tried to divorce him. And I never knew, never had a clue that he was a recovering alcoholic. Then I thought about the little subtle remarks he'd say like, live and let live, first things first, keep it simple and easy does it. Yes those are all AA slogans now that I think about it. There were people from his AA meeting at the funeral. Now I know what the Sunday night business meeting was really about.

I was beginning to wonder who H.C. really was, because so much that I didn't know was coming to light now. I think back to the times and trouble I used to have with money when I lived back in Los Angeles, back before I met H.C. Things have sure changed for me since then, and to think, I didn't want to come back home to old boring Memphis. Never thought I would find my one and only true love right here in Tennessee. Back in L.A. my bank account was always overdrawn. I was struggling from paycheck to paycheck, juggling bills, trying to keep the mortgage and daycare paid, always borrowing money from somebody. My brother use to say money runs from you. H.C. helped me become more financially responsible and stable. I don't know what I would have done without him. One thing I did know for sure was that he was my love. I knew I would truly, truly miss him. And now, I had no choice but to go on. Here I was ten years later, forty years old and alone, because I chose to live my life a secret, with the man of my dreams. Why did we hafta be a secret?

After I purchased our house on Pecan Grove Lane, I had just about $15,000 left. It was enough to get by until I found a job, as no incidents came along. Which you know they did. However, H.C. talked me into transferring the settlement money that I was awarded into a money market account versus just my checking account. He said, "This way, Sweetheart, you will have some money that's not too easily accessible for you and perhaps it will make a little interest." At first I was insulted, then I thought, "Why not. Lord knows I've let too much money slip thru my hands and nothing to show for it." I found a job as a court reporter, and H.C. made sure that I saved 50 percent of my check. He paid close attention to every penny I spent.

After about one year he told me that he loved me, and that he would make sure I never, ever forgot him. He promised he'd never let me go. He said he was really impressed with how I had caught on to this managing money thing. When I met H.C.my credit score was three hundred, and now it's eight fifty. I pay for things that I need as well as what I want, for me and the kids without strain, not just because I can. I even own a few shares of stock that have been bringing in a little profit. H.C. hardly let me pay for a thing once I was financially stable enough to do so. When I tried to pay for our dinners or whatever he'd always say, "Baby, save your money and remember all we've got is one day at a time."

I remember how he used to say, "If we don't go first class, Baby, we don't go." I missed him and there would be no other man in life like him.

The week after the funeral I was getting ready to leave the house, when a FedEx truck pulled up, and the courier brought me an envelope. Strange. I hadn't ordered anything lately. It was addressed to me from the law office of Charles and Smitt, P. C. I was surprised, because I thought no one in H.C.'s office was aware of our relationship. What could this be, and who knows me from that office?

When I opened the package there was a legal document for me to sign, along with a letter:

"In order for us to close this estate, please sign the attached sworn affidavit upon receipt of this document before a notary and return it back to us in the prepaid FedEx envelope."

Attached to the letter was a check for $500,000, made out to me, along with the deeds to my house and our special place in Jackson, and the title to my Jaguar and CTS. The mortgage and cars had been paid off. Oh, my God! He never forgot me. Did his law partner know about me? Did his wife know about me? I knew about her, but no one has ever said a word to me in our entire ten-year secret.

I don't really need anything right now, except another H.C.I have enough money for my daily expenses, savings in the bank, and money put away for the girls' college educations. So I have no need to touch it.

But you know, some of my girlfriends are still struggling with their money problems. I would still be in the same shape, too, if I had listened to my best friend, my hater friend.

She said, "I wouldn't give myself to no white man."

She kept saying, "He's using you. He thinks we're back in the old days, don't he? He thinks he owns you. He just wants some free black pussy."

I almost listened to her. I came close so many times to just letting him go, listening to her broke ass. She always tried to find out what our sex life was like, but I would never tell. She tried all kinds of ways to make me talk with her about it.

She would say, "I hear white boys have small dicks. Is that true?"

I told her I don't know about white boys, just one white man.

Then she'd say, "I hear they give great head."

And I said, "Most men do, don't they?"

She'd laugh and say, "Girl, I can't get you to tell me a damn thing about that white boy of yours. Stop being so secretive. I bet he's got a wife, and he sure must be ugly, 'cause no one has seen him." I just let her talk.

I wonder if I will ever find another man as good as H.C. Since he passed away, the days have been so long and so lonely. I guess you can't have it all. I'm just glad I have my book club to help me relieve some of the tension in my life. Thanks to H.C., membership and dues is no financial strain.

BECKY

The ten of us had been meeting for three years now. We called it the book club.

Many of us were happily married…umm…or so you could say. And, in the book club, we get together and discuss the latest book that we've all read. We all read the same book and got together on the last Friday of every month to discuss it. Every one brought a dish and we would go from there. At least that's what we'd say before we left home.

We met from seven p.m. until eleven p.m. That gave everyone a chance to get back home by midnight or so.

Take I-240 East, heading towards Nashville. Merge to I-40 Nashville, to US 64e to 15E. Then exit 18 towards Somerville/Bolivar, to Collierville Arlington Road. Take the first left on Jefferson and five minutes down to 1069 Jefferson. I knew this route with my eyes closed. I am sure everyone else did, too. The book club had been my best day every month for the last three years.

When we got here, everything was all set up. The guys arrived around eight p.m. and Rainbow, our limousine driver, had never been late. Rainbow was one of only two other people who knew our secret, he and Ms. Phyllis. She kept every room in this house beautiful for us. Jernethia hired an interior decorator named Ms. Mary Jane Jones and she designed everything.

Mary Jane was getting kinda nosy and mentioned how she would love to join the book club if we had room for one more member. I knew better. Never mix business with pleasure. That could cause trouble. Plus, I heard from some of her associates and past clients that she's great at what she does, but don't even think about having her around on any other level. She likes Valium mixed with wine a little too much on the regular. So I informed her, "Sorry, no room for any more members, but we'll keep you in mind and let you know if we get an opening."

Most of us were old friends from childhood, and we were quite particular about meeting people outside of our circle. Mary Jane knew her stuff. This place was laid out… We had beds by Thomasville, Panama, Italian leather sofas. The walls had beautiful art prints, and a few tasteful original pieces, as well. The lighting was just right, vaulted ceilings, skylights and the sound system played smooth jazz. There were unique chaise lounges. There was no room left undone; each room had a different theme and was perfect all the way.

We set it up so there was one guy for each of us. We had a total of twenty guys on a rotating basis so the ten we saw one month would not be the same ten next month. Every other month you might see the same guy, but never two months in a row. When we first decided to make this happen, we all wrote down what kind of man we would just love to have. Not to marry, just have for fun. As Luther Vandross would say, "If only for one night."Or like that old school song by the Dells, "I'm just shopping, not buying anything!" We also had a couple of young ladies, for variety.

At our first meeting, we made a list of guidelines for our guests. We also gave Ms. Phyllis a list of things to do and what we wanted to keep on hand at all times. We gave her updated instructions after we meet on Fridays each month. That gave her a month to gather everything before the next meeting and she never missed a beat. She always had everything we asked for, and in all the right places.

Supply List:

1. Dental dams

2. Condoms

3. KY Warming Jelly

4. Silver Bullets

5. Body butter

6. Almond oil from Europe

7. Large soy candles

8. Yankee Candles (fragrances matching the seasons)

9. Eucalyptus, chocolate, strawberry and vanilla/lavender bath soak

10. Shea butter

11. Baby oil

12. Hand held and back massagers

13. Negro, Moët and Chandon, Dom Perignon, and Crystal

14. Chardonnay, Gewürztraminer, Liebfraumilch, and Merlot

15. Grey Goose, Crown Black, Remy VSOP, Ciroc, Glenlivet, Pierre Ferrand, and Johnny Walker Blue

16. Twenty satin pillowcases (red, black and white)

17. Twenty terrycloth his and her robes (white only)

18. New candle holders and gold and silver snuffers

19. Gevalia Coffee

20. Truffles in assorted flavors

21. Cigars from Cuba

22. Ten sets of The New Hotel 800-thread-count sheets.

23. Last but not least, don't forget to check with Neville to see what kind of supplies he may need for the massage area.

24. When it's time to stock up for the winter, call Mr. Parker, the log man, to see when we can expect to get wood.

Some of the rules for our guests were:

(a)Never ask personal questions. Not our real names, ages, where we live, or what our profession is. Do not ask if we have kids, husbands, or pets. Do not even ask how we want it.

(b)Don't speak or acknowledge any one of us anywhere except at the book club.

(c) Come in with a smile, take care of business, and shut the fuck up.

(d)Read the card files. There is one for each of us with our club name and preferences. Here you will find how to please us. Favorite colors, scents, fabrics—everything is there.

(e) Pay close attention to what type of cologne each woman wants on her man.

We each pledged ten thousand dollars to get started, which gave us a total of one hundred thousand sitting in our kitty. Group dues were paid once per year, five thousand each. That added fifty thousand per year. We spent five thousand for entertainment and two thousand five hundred a month for lease, maintenance and accessories. Ms. Phyllis, our cleaning lady and caretaker, was the best and we paid her well, not only for cleaning, but for knowing how to keep a secret. And she had a great time, too.

The men we had were the best, Grade A, USDA finest. Just like top of the line beef, we had a Rainbow Coalition going on! Ha... ha. They all looked good and smelled good. No fat stomachs. No boring ass conversations about themselves, like what we heard at home. You know, like, "Back in the day how I used to, what I used to do when I was twenty, or how I used to be able to wet them up in my day." No gray hairs, no wrinkles, no implants, no dentures, and no one over the age of forty. These guys knew exactly how to make us girls feel good, and that was what was required. They were the best, and we never settled for less. We paid for it, too.

They each had a specialty. To name a few: Neville, the masseur; Cody, the well endowed; Phillip, the great kisser; Jonathan, the affectionate lover; David, the rough and wild beast; Samuel, the sexy six-pack, Boyd, the teaser; Basil, the tongue pleaser; and, of course, we also have Sylvia and Joann. They were on call on an as needed basis. Never knew what one of our book club girls might need.

Need it? Want it? We had it! When one of our guys had his forty-first birthday, we celebrated with him and bid him farewell. In the three years that we'd been meeting we'd only had to replace two.

To me, it seemed as if the twenty-five-year-olds are the most fun. They'd just discovered that pleasing beats teasing any day. The thirty-year-olds had finally learned the right techniques, and at forty, they could take care of you easily. As the song by Anthony David says, "I can do it with my eyes closed." It came natural for them now, just like riding a bike, and everything on them still worked exceptionally well.

At the beginning of each meeting, we stated our oath in unison, and it went like this:

We gather here the last Friday of each month at the same time

to come together and have a great time!

We know what we do is pretty bold!

But that's the way it is when your love life's getting old!

So relax, kick back, and, oh boy, enjoy your Toy.

We all have one common goal and that is to never, ever tell another soul!

Then the ten of us stood in a circle and I took Valerie's hand and said, "Your secret's safe with me."

She then grabbed Jessica's hand and said, "Your secret's safe with me."

We continued this ritual one by one. Jessica grabbed Faye's hand, Faye grabbed Foy's hand, Foy grabbed Rose's hand, Rose grabbed Renee's hand, Renee grabbed Mabel's hand, Mabel grabbed Yolanda's hand, and, finally, Yolanda grabbed Jernethia's hand. Once we were all holding hands, in unison we said, "Enjoy!"

Every guy or lady was paid immediately at the end of the evening. Ms. Phyllis was always glad to pass out the envelopes as they departed, and we always paid cash.

The book club had everything we needed. You see, although some of us were happily married to the right man, he no longer was, or never was, the right man when it came to pleasing us in the bedroom. Not the one for saying the right things the way we wanted to hear it. No sensitivity. You know, things like, "Baby, you smell so good," or "That dress looks nice on you," or "Let me rub your back, Baby, or your feet, or brush your hair," or "I want to shave your legs for you. I could polish your toe nails for you, Baby." It's the small things, phrases like, "Baby, please let me rub you down." Oh, we could go on and on. After so many years of trying this and that and nothing worked, we'd all given up and settled and knew this was just the way it was.

Damned old women, who have been married a long, long time. When we were young girls, they never told us this secret! Never told what they really had to give up to stay married so long, but now we knew. I bet some of them had some kind of club back in their day, too. I knew we're not the only ones. Can't be the only women to have thought of this shit. We'd all spent way too much time, invested too much to leave our husbands. And, for what? The book club was just what the doctor ordered. Actually, we thought it was the best thing since sliced bread.

The house was owned by Ms. Luizer. She was Mabel's mom, but as far as Ms. Luizer knew, Ms. Phyllis was the renter. She just sent our monthly rent by mail to some post office box in zip code 37042. It looked like a large two story mansion sitting back off the street. It sat vacant for two years before we rented it, so I just bet Ms. Luizer was pleased. The funny thing is, Ms. Luizer was probably giving Mabel the money to pay the dues!

The way it got started was that Valerie and I used to meet and talk about how nice it would be to have a man to do just what and how we wanted. She'd had such bad luck when it comes to men. She used to say her picker was broke; she always had made bad men decisions. We talked about how nice it would be to have a fun place for all of us girlfriends to meet and then we finally got it.

Jernethia's husband passed away a few years back and she said, "Oh, no, never again. I'm free, Sweetheart. No more damned husbands. Way too much work."

Now, Rose, why was it we always had to fight with Rose? She never wanted to go home. She was always the one who ended up a little too tipsy, a little too loud, a little too needy. She wanted to fall in love with every one of them that she slept with, always crying. A couple of times, the group wanted to put her out of the club and replace her with someone else, but after three years, we just didn't want to chance bringing in someone new. Besides, that kind of drama could come back to haunt us.

Once Rose wanted us to let her have both the women at the same time. She said she wanted a threesome. That night she was so fucked up, we had to leave her at the house and pay Ms. Phyllis extra to stay with her overnight. That damned Rose, she could be a hellcat once she had too much to drink, or should we say, once she got too happy. She would get loud and start talking about how she loved them two damn girls, how they knew how to make it right for her. She wanted to give details and we never, ever talked openly about what went on behind those closed doors.

But Rose, Rose was a lush and she loved being a lush. I think the last two times we met, we had the most trouble out of her. She was drunk as a skunk, and I found out why later. She'd found out that the Reverend had been sleeping with one of his younger members at the church who was a choir member and it had been going on for quite some time. Right under her nose. Everyone knew except her. She was really hurt and upset about that.

The rest of us were pretty content and stable; however, we had found a way to replace the missing link, which was that feeling of pleasure. Our motto was called the Three F's: Find Them, Fool Them, and Fuck Them.

Never once did we have any problems with the guys. No, I take that back. We had a problem with Samuel. He saw Yolanda at the Aretha Franklin concert with her husband. Just walked right over; he was with some little young ass girl and started talking like they were old friends.

Ugh! Unacceptable. The next month we met him at the door and got rid of his ass. Guess he forgot the rules, "Don't speak or acknowledge any one of us anywhere except at the book club." I know it got back to the other guys, but it was never mentioned, and none of us ever had a problem like that again.

MABEL

I'd been planning to go visit my cousin Lynn for the past few weeks, and this seemed like a good evening to ride over there and show her my new red Cadillac. Besides, I wanted to pump her for some information on her personal life. I figured maybe we could take a dip in her pool and catch up on girl talk.

Lynn had this secret relationship going on and no one had seen this guy yet. I figured she'd been seeing him for about six months now. I knew she had a very successful life out there in Fayette County. She'd been on the bench in Circuit Court now for the past ten years. She had finally found a guy that she was in love with, and I was happy for her. Maybe I'd get a cousin-in-law after all. I kept asking her, "When am I going to meet this special person?"

It was always, "I promise to come by soon, Mabel." She was frequently working or gone somewhere out of the country.

When I pulled up to her house I saw her Boxer was in the driveway, with its license plate that says, BI-N-BY. Her house is so beautiful. It's sitting on 1. 36 acres, 1645 Woodbridge Road, Somerville, Tennessee. She says it only takes her fifteen to twenty minutes to get to work. Everyone knows her in this little town. The oval shaped pool in back and the screened in deck are awesome. It's so peaceful out here. I told her, "It's so quiet, you can hear a mouse take a piss on a cotton ball."

All I heard right then were the birds chirping and the waterfall out back where she has a fishpond.

Momma was always saying she wished Lynn would get married at least once and have a little baby before she gets too old. She knew not to expect any grandbabies from me. Momma says marriage isn't for everybody, but she feels like everyone should at least give it one shot.

I was trying to remember, what was that guy's name she used to see from Murfreesboro? Calvin, Calvin... no, let's see, now. No. It was Devin Brooks. I thought he was nice, but she broke it off with him and broke his heart. She said she didn't want to see him anymore after dating him for three years. I thought he was a great young man, but I guess not the right one for her.

Anyway, I was glad to see she'd got something new going on. She was always taking vacations—Paris, Canada, Costa Rica, Dubai, the Cayman Islands. Dubai seems to be her favorite place lately. She always brought back great gifts, never forgot to bring something nice for Momma and me. I thought she'd said this year she was planning a trip to Italy with her new secret love.

Hum. This Range Rover probably belonged to the mystery man.

I got out of my car and, as I approached the door to ring the bell, it was already open. I thought to myself, "This house is really too big to be leaving doors open, someone could walk in and she wouldn't hear a thing. Guess she feels pretty safe out here. The way her house sits off the road, if you didn't know her, you would have no need to even come this way."

I went in and all I could hear was panting, moaning sounds, and soft, soft, whimpers. I could also hear XM Satellite Radio. The station was Watercolors. I know that station anywhere 'cause that's what I keep my radio tuned, too. Sounded like a song by Najee. I came into the foyer and saw no one. Then I turned the corner and still no one.

When I looked up the spiral staircase that led to her sitting area, there they were! Hugging and kissing, and more shocking than that, who I saw with her! I was embarrassed; I felt flushed. At first I couldn't quite see him, his back was to me and he was on his knees. When he turned his head around, he was a she. Her long wavy hair, which was usually pinned up in a bun, hung down the sides of her face. It was Dr. Homer, our family OBGYN. Just about everyone in our family, females that is, were patients of hers. She'd delivered everyone's babies in the family. And here she was with her lips pressed up against my cousin. She had to be fifteen years older than Lynn.

What a shocker; so many secrets in this damn place. I quietly eased back out the door, got in my car, and drove away. This was way too much to handle right now. All the way home, all I could think of was what I'd just seen. Dr. Homer and my cousin together? Here I was thinking she had some new guy and all the time it was old ass, gay ass, dyke ass, Dr. Homer. I heard that she's bi-sexual, likes girls and boys, but I never believed it. Never gave any of us in the family any reason to suspect or question what she was. I can say she does know a lot about pussies first hand.

Well, you know what they say. Whatever blows your dress up! Lynn seemed so happy now. I wondered if her dad or mom knew what's really going on. Well, she was grown and at her age she could really do damn well what she pleased. I would call her later. When I made it home the first thing I was gonna do was pour myself a good stiff drink. This had blown my mind.

DANA

I sat there staring at those two boxes. One more still to go. I decided to get a cup of coffee to drink while I worked. No, changed my mind. Let's make that Jack Daniels instead. This is just too much information to grasp all at once for me, especially sober. My God, papers from Sears to stockholders, old savings bonds, cash, life insurance policies, one from Mutual of Omaha, another from Prudential—all listing me as the beneficiary. I shook my head and totaled them all up. Three hundred seventy-five thousand dollars. Oh, my Lord.

What was I supposed to do now? Did I tell my sisters, or so-called sisters, or just keep it all to myself? Those two had been mean to me all my life…

Oh, hell. There was also a small note pad that had a little poem written on it.

Got a little secret here in Tennessee
and the holder of this key will
certainly learn a little bit more about me!
I never ever told a single soul
what key number A-23 will unfold.
731 N. Tipton, 38019

Where in the heck was 38019? I needed to look up that zip code to see what city that could be. I felt like I was on a scavenger hunt.

I moved the boxes back in the corner by the window. I went to my laptop and signed on. I Googled the zip code, and 38019 is Covington, Tennessee. Now what in the heck was she doing way out there? I typed the address in my Garmin and it gave an estimated time for travel of about forty-five minutes. It was the beginning of fall and the leaves were beginning to change. Tomorrow the temperature was supposed to be about seventy-eight degrees.

I was in a daze the rest of the day. Couldn't turn off all the thoughts going through my head. I tried watching some television. Then I fed my birds, but I just couldn't shut off my head. All kinds of thoughts running through my head. I decided I would stay in the rest of the day. I did my usual; cleaned house, listened to my music, talked to a few friends on the phone. I prepared myself some dinner and took a soak.

About eight-thirty p.m. I took a quick look outside my window. I always like to check out my surroundings. A Hummer limo was pulling in slowly next door. The last time I saw that limo was about a month ago. I wondered what really goes on at that house. Most of the time it was pretty still over there. That house had been empty for a long time. Seemed like people were coming there about once a month, that's it. Maybe it was being used as some kind of vacation house or something. Well as long as no one bothered me, I would just mind my own business and stay out of theirs.

I climbed in bed around ten p.m. I tossed and turned for quite a while, until I finally got up and fixed myself another Jack Daniels, and that did the trick. The next thing I knew, it was morning. Actually, late morning. It was ten a.m. The sun was shining. I got up and tried to get myself together. I looked outside and my baby blue Thunderbird was just sitting out there waiting for me. I shook my head to clear it. "I think I will let the top down today. I need to get as much air as I can. There's no telling what secrets this key will unlock."

Let's see, I had the key, had my Garmin…wait, I needed some music to ride with. I decided on Randy Travis and Rascal Flats. Once I was on the road, I began to get excited. When I was almost there the Garmin said, "Turn left then turn right. Proceed to destination on left."

I thought, "Hmm. Nothing over here but moving and storage places."

The address of the place I was going had a big security gate and you needed a code for access. I thought, "Now what? I don't have a code, only this key."

The keyboard said press #3 for assistance. An Asian-sounding lady said, "May I help you?"

I told her that I was here to go inside of a storage room for my deceased mother and that I only had a key and the storage room number. She asked, "What was your mother's name?"

I told her Cherry Esienberg or Cherry Davis, and she said, "Give me one minute and I will look that up for you."

I waited about five minutes even though it seemed like forever. Then she said, "Who are you now? What is your name, Honey?"

I told her Dana Davis and she said as the gate opened, "Go ahead, ma'am. You are listed as an authorized user."

Another surprise. Now I wondered what would be in store for me when I get to this storage room. All the storage room doors in this whole place were green. You know, like a winter green. The color you often see on a lot of shutters on houses.

Now there was a sign: For storage rooms A-C, turn left. D-E, turn right.

Okay, left it is! I pulled up and when I saw that lock, old and rusted, I thought, "Wonder how long she's had this storage?"

My heart started beating fast and my legs felt wobbly, but I got out anyhow. There wasn't another soul around; I could hear myself breathing. I could hear the echo of every step I took and my palms had even started to sweat. I don't think that's happened to me since I had to speak in school at graduation. Okay, I took a deep breath, ready to unlock this damn thing and see just what other secrets my mom had hidden from me all of these years.

Oh my God! The first thing I noticed is that she had this whole place fixed up like someone's living room. She had pictures on the wall, coffee table and end tables, lamp, and a baby grand piano. I couldn't believe it! She had pictures of herself and this man all snuggled up together. She had baby pictures of herself in black and white from way back when, pictures of me, pictures of Uncle Walter and Aunt Cora and two little girls.

I just couldn't figure out who that man was with her. They had pictures from a cruise ship, Norwegian Cruise Lines, for a trip to Alaska. I never knew she went on a cruise. Memorabilia from Las Vegas, New Orleans, Niagara Falls, Mexico, and some places that looked like they were somewhere in Tennessee, by the look of the trees, but I didn't know where. A lot of the pictures were recent, not like the old black and white ones I'd found in the box at the house.

Wow! I had to sit down. This was tripping me out. Then I saw the box on the coffee table. I opened the box. It was an old jewelry box, you know, the kind that you don't see much anymore. It had a little gold key to turn it open. There were three drawers and when I opened it, it played a tune. It was the music to that song, "You are my sunshine, my only sunshine. You make me happy when skies are grey." There was a little ballerina in white spinning around.

The room became so silent to me for that moment when the song was playing. It seemed as if I could feel my mommy right there with me. In that box was a letter, and when I unfolded it, there was her familiar handwriting:

To my one and only beloved daughter, Dana,

I love you very much. You turned out to be a wonderful daughter and the reason that I went and got your two sisters is because I didn't want you to grow up alone. The doctor said they almost lost me bringing you into the world and I could never, ever, have another child. Your sisters, as you probably know by now, are your cousins. Your father, Robert Davis, is living over in Mason County with the woman he left me for, his secretary. Maybe one day you might want to look him up. That's up to you. I did my best. My brother, your Uncle Walter, and his wife should have never been allowed to have children.

But you know, God has a way of fixing things. And when they sent their mother off to jail, I knew it wouldn't be long before your uncle joined her. He always was a good-for-nothing man; he was a good-for-nothing boy growing up. I tried to tell your Aunt Cora, but she was in love. Just adored and worshiped the ground he walked on. A lot of girls fell for him. It was that blonde hair and blue eyes, and that damn dimple in his chin that drove them crazy. I could go on and on about the women he messed over. My momma worshiped the ground he walked on. He could never do no wrong in her eyes. But, she finally got to see the real him when he got his wife in trouble and she took the blame for something that I think he had a lot to do with. That was when she started to hate him for real. Oh, he was a charmer.

The pictures you see around the wall are great memories of me and Bud. This is the man who I loved so much and he loved me. I never married him out of fear, afraid that I would fall in love again, trust and be hurt. So we had a never-ending secret life that went on from the first day I met him until…until my dying day, if you're reading this. He watched you grow up from a distance and I made him promise to never, ever, tell, and I never ever told, except on this letter now to you.

Now it's up to you. I hope one day that you find a love like mine that will last you forever, until your dying day. If you are reading this letter, I know you have found the key and you are sitting here in my most favorite secret place in the whole wide world, the place where all of my secrets have been revealed to you.

Do as you wish. Share it with someone you trust or just keep it a secret. Tell your sisters, I mean cousins. Share the money with them if you wish, but I'm sure you've seen just how they act towards each other and towards you, now that I'm gone. The choice is yours. My things that are here in this storage, that's up to you. You can leave them there, never pay for storage space again, and eventually they will auction everything off. You can take them home with you and one day share my secret with someone you trust, but take what you like. The only thing I ask that you keep, other than all the things that will give you a few dollars, is…. take a look in the last drawer of this jewelry box. There should be a 5-karat diamond ring. I want you to keep it and, if you ever have a daughter, give it to her as remembrance of me, her grandmother.

I love you always,

Your Mommy

I couldn't seem to stop crying. Tears were just rolling out of my eyes like a faucet that has a slow leak. Why did she leave me with all of this information? How could she keep such a secret for so, so long?

As I dried my tears and walked towards my car, I could hear the echo of every step I made. I took my camera out of the back seat and carried it back inside the storage room. I took a picture of each and every item in this room. I would never forget this room. Never. I wondered, "Should I look for the man in the pictures? What can he tell me about my mommy? What secrets does he know about her that I don't know?"

Now just one more picture of the jewelry box, then I picked it up and carried it out to my car. One last look back. Wow, my mommy. Now I know the meaning of keeping a secret and taking it all the way to your dying day.

I put my camera and the jewelry box on my front seat as I backed away from the storage room. Then I turned around and headed for the office. I didn't see the lady right away. She was bending down working on something. I got out of my car and as I was walking towards her, she was walking towards me. She had a box of Kleenex tissues and she passed me a few. The tears started flowing again. She was crying and so was I; we gave each other a big hug. She looked like she could have been around my mommy's age. I gave her the key and said, "I will never come back here again. I will send the piano movers out to get the piano. The rest of the stuff is yours."

As I headed back toward I-40 East, I thought, "Mommy, may she rest in peace." I always wondered why she never brought any man around us. Wondered, "Didn't she ever have a desire to have a man friend?"

Now I know. She never showed interest in any of the men that tried to flirt with her. Always seemed so content just tending to us girls, watching TV, crocheting blankets all the time, and just going to Bingo on Wednesday nights. Maybe, just maybe, I will look up that man I saw in those pictures. I'm sure he can tell me some more stuff about my mommy that I don't know.

BECKY

I called the clubhouse around eleven a.m. on a Saturday morning to check in with Ms. Phyllis. The phone just rang and rang and no one answered. I started worrying that something was wrong. After a few minutes, I called again. This time Ms. Phyllis answered on the third ring.

I said, "Hey girl, it's Becky. Is Rose still there? Did she manage to get it together and get out of there before she had too much explaining to do when she got home to the Reverend?"

"Hell, no," Phyllis said, "Rose is soaking in the Jacuzzi with the music playing loud. She took a bottle of Johnny Walker Blue in with her and hasn't come out! I think she's getting fucked up all over again. Keeps telling me to call Joann to come over, and you know we don't do business here on Saturdays. Girl, what do you want me to do? I hate to just leave her, but I need to get back home. I have something to do this evening. I called the Reverend for her this morning and explained to him that she and I were doing some redecorating at the club house, so instead of her coming home last night she decided to stay. Otherwise, she would have to turn around and come right back. He thanked me for calling, but didn't seem to be too concerned if you ask me! Like he was up to something himself. Jackass. That's why Rose is the way she is now."

"Okay. Look, can you just stay until I can get back out there? Give me an hour and a half. Let's see, it's eleven -thirty now. I'll be there at one p.m."

"All right, but if you're not here by one p.m. on the dot, I'm rolling out. I hafta go. I'll leave her drunk ass here, Becky."

"Damn, damn. That Rose is getting so out of control. We are going to have to address this at the next meeting and come up with some kind of solution once and for all."

I got out there at exactly one p.m. and, when I pulled up, I could hear the music playing from inside the house. That means it must've been really loud. Normally you can't hear a thing from the outside of this big place. That was one of the many features we all loved about our clubhouse. When I opened the door Phyllis met me.

"Rose finally came out of the bathroom, but she is walking around dancing and crying. She's smoking and singing and got the CD player on repeat, playing the same damn 'Tired' song over and over and over again.

"I'm outta here Becky, you can take over now."

When Rose saw me, she said, "Hey, Becky girl! I don't think I can ever go back." Her makeup had left dark circles and smudges all over her face from crying, her hair was all matted and standing up all over her head. I could even see her weave tracks. "I can't do this anymore. Not at home. Not at church. Not around my kids. I'm so tired of playing these games. I don't like the lie I've been living, and I'm tired of drinking about it, shopping about it, sleeping about it, lying about it, and acting as if I don't see it. I've known for a very long time, but I settled for it because of the wonderful lifestyle it brought me and the kids. Now that they are all grown and gone and living their own lives, I can't stand it anymore. I've worked for Shelby County long enough and I think I'll go ahead and retire and move.

"I've had just about as much of this bullshit life as I can take. I'm way past my retirement and I think it's time I let go. So please, please, Beck, if you're really my friend, help me get outta here. And I don't mean just from the book club, or my home. I mean this whole town. I've done my homework, even though you bitches think I just stay drunk all the time. I know what I am about to tell you is against our rules, but I have been seeing Joann outside of the club meeting night. I plan to take her with me out to my new home in the country. I love her and I know that we can have a nice and peaceful life there. It's just a little bit past Franklin. What I need from you is to help me find someone to help me get my things from that damn house while he's not there."

She continued, "I think Monday is going to be my best day. You know the Reverend runs around all day on Mondays taking care of church business, plus he'll have extra work with all the gifts and money that he'll take in from Sunday. He will be gone all day and I'm sure he will disappear on through the evening with that girl and call it night service. I'm ready. Do you still have the number for that young guy who used to come out to the club last year?"

"Well you gotta be a little more specific than that, Rose. We had a lot of young guys, oops, I mean new books, last year. Which one?"

"Let's see, I think his name was Melvin. You remember him. The one with the lips tattooed on his stomach," she giggled.

"Ha. Ha. Boy, do I ever!" He claimed he had a moving company and that was just one of the many things he did, or so he said. I paused and focused my gaze on Rose, "Girl, are you sure that this is what you want to do?"

"I'm positive, and I should've done it long ago."

"Okay, if this will make you happy, then I'm willing to help in any way I can. I'll call Phyllis and have her pull his file and I'll give him a call."

"Thanks," she took my hand, "And, Becky, it's for the best. I don't want to get out somewhere, get wasted, and start talking and end up telling our secret."

"Let me try and get Phyllis right now; she has an emergency list that she can get to," I said. I dialed her number, "Hey, Phyllis, this is Becky. I hate to bother you, but this is an emergency. Can you look in your special file and find me a number? Should be listed as Melvin Lips."

"Okay, girl, hold on. Found him. He left us August last year, "she said.

"I know, but we need his number for something else. I can't go into details right now. I'll explain later."

"Okay. His number is 931-374-9865."

I called Melvin as soon as I got off the phone with Phyllis." Hi, Melvin. This is Becky," I said," You used to do some private work for me and a few ladies last year and someone mentioned that you have a moving service. Are you still in the business?"

"Yes. Now who did you say you were?"

"Becky, exit 64, the clubhouse girls."

"Oh…Oh…yes…how you doing, Baby?"

"Listen, I need a big favor. One of our members has an emergency situation and needs someone to move her ASAP, as in yesterday, you know what I mean? Would you be available to move her in say…two days? We will definitely pay you for your time and for giving you such short notice. She's going towards Franklin, Tennessee. Ever been there? It's about 100 miles from here. Can you get over to her place Sunday and take a look at what she needs moving? I think it'll probably take at least two guys to get everything."

"Sure, I can do that for you ladies. Let me get a hold of my guys and once I come out Sunday, I'll be able to give you a price."

"Okay, how about around ten a.m. on Sunday? I asked.

Rose was in the background waving her hands and mouthing, "No. No. Not ten. Make it nine."

"Forget ten. Can you come at nine? Great. It's 4025 Farrington. Thanks, Melvin, we owe you one."

"You owe me. You don't owe me. Did you forget who I am and my motto? My name is Mel and everything is swell, 'cause I aim to please."

"Well thank you, Mel. We'll see you soon." I hung up." Whew. Okay, we got that straight. Now Rose, how in the hell are you gonna pull this off?"

"I'll just fake it like I always do."

I laughed, "Why nine a.m.?"

"The Reverend leaves for church at eight and the service starts at eleven, so he won't be back. You know he's gotta run everything."

"Rose, everything is all set. Now let's get some coffee in you, so you can get cleaned up and go home. You know you have a big day tomorrow and you want things to go smoothly," I told her.

Rose said, "Okay, I can do this."

She had sobered up after her second cup of coffee. She gathered herself, cleaned up her face and hair, grabbed her things and headed for the door.

"Wait for me, girl," I said, "Don't leave me. I came back out here for you."

"Sorry Becky. So much on my mind."

I gave her a big hug, set the alarm, and we walked out together. She took one look back at the house and said, "I'm gonna miss this place. Best secret in town. Becky, please explain to the group for me. I hafta go, for my own sanity."

"I understand, Rose, but you've made us lose an employee. We need to find another girl to take Joann's place. Quick, fast, and in a hurry. Maybe not as good as Joann, though. She makes people fall in love and leave and shit! Just kidding, girl. You'd better be glad I love ya, and that we've been friends since junior high. Now tell me, who in the hell can we let new into our club? It's just been us ten for the last three years. Why you hafta go off and leave? Who in the hell am I going to find who knows how to keep a secret like ours?"

All the way on the drive back home, I kept thinking about poor Rose. I never knew it was so bad, so hard on her. I thought about sending all the girls a text message when I got home, but I couldn't wait. This was an emergency. I sent it right away, "BRIEF EMERGENCY CLUB MEETING SCHEDULED AT 6 P.M.TODAY. STARBUCKS.EAST LOCATION. BCNU!"

We never meet all together in town. We've never all been seen together, that is, not in town. It won't be any different this time. First, Valerie, Jessica, and Jernethia showed, and as they came in and saw me, I just said, "No more Rose, she's gone. See you at the next meeting. Think of who can replace her."

At six-thirty, Mabel, Yolanda, and Renee came in, and I repeated what I'd just said to the other three. "Rose is gone. See you at the next meeting. Think of who can replace her."

Finally, Faye and Foy came in. They are partners and always late for everything. I said the same to them. They were shocked. Foy said, "You shittin me!" She started to giggle.

"No. She's gone for good. Think of who could replace her and let me know at our next meeting."

I didn't want to get into the details. Those two were so excited, but I felt like I'd just lost a sister.

I could tell Rose was fed up, and I couldn't blame her. One thing, cheating on me behind my back and I never catch you, but to cheat on me right in front of my face…that was unacceptable. Rose never did like to fight. I remember I always had to speak up for her at school. Someone was always bullying her. Stealing her lunch money, her sweater, her books, but not me. I wasn't having it. Once I got in a fight with this boy named Ronnie for her. They had been dating and he was talking shit about how she wasn't this or that. He got loud right during lunchtime in the cafeteria and every one was looking and listening. He slapped her and knocked her wig off. Everyone was laughing and I came up behind him and knocked him down on the ground so fast that he didn't know what hit him. I said, "Don't you ever mess over my friend. She doesn't want you anyway." I paused and looked him in the eyes, "Besides, I hear you got a pencil dick."

Everybody started laughing and he cried. We never had any more problems out of him. Maybe that's why she fell for Joann. Joann was tough, but very feminine. She was pretty and gentle, yet rough at the same time. I guessed that's what she needed right now. I hoped she would stay happy forever.

Me, I was just fine. Thank the Lord for our book club. I was a block from my house now and wondering what that boring ass husband of mine was doing. Probably his usual, sitting on the couch with a bowl of nuts beside him and some beer watching the Western Channel. He worked ninety-eight percent of the time, and the other two percent he was boring as hell. Still, you had to love him. I'd never wanted for anything since the day we married. He was my fifth husband and, before we met, I didn't think God put any more good men on earth. I thought they all left with my dad, and my girlfriend's dads, but I found out there are still a few good men. I was really shocked to find a good one in Tennessee.

I've learned that it's a lot of crazies in this place. Memphis, I found out, had the most. Then I found out it ain't just Memphis. They got crazy ones everywhere around here—Gatlinburg, Johnson City, Knoxville, and Lebanon, just to name a few. Must be something in the water? Or maybe the milk, when they were first born.

When I got in the house, there he was, watching his cowboy channel, drinking beer with a glass of Crown Royal on the side. I asked, "Baby, do you want to do anything special this evening?"

"Naw, just my usual Saturday Night Special," he grinned.

Saturday night special consists of me cooking fried catfish, corn on the cob, coleslaw, and fried potatoes. Afterwards, I dress up in my sexy night wear with matching stilettos and my long sexy lace front wig. I get all made up to dance and swing around that pole he put up in the bedroom. After my twenty-minute performance, we have ten minutes of sex and his ass falls asleep. That party usually starts at nine p.m. and ends by ten. My post-coital routine, once he is asleep and snoring, is to curl up on my favorite beautiful chase lounge, read, listen to my favorite music on my iPod, and maybe talk on the phone.

SARA

I decided I'd better start planning what I want to do once I got my money. With me, it was usually save, save, save. This time I was gonna spend, spend, spend. I'd been saving all of my life. No telling how much life I might have left, so I thought, I'm just gonna get busy. I made a list of who, when, and what I was gonna do. First thing I was gonna do was buy that lady who lives in the house behind me a divorce from that bastard she's been with for so many years. I had heard how mean he'd been to her for more than twenty years. I'd heard him hitting on her, heard her crying, cursing, getting cursed out, seen her looking sad and bad, yet she had never left. Throughout the years we had had an occasion or two to talk woman to woman, and she had asked me to please not say anything to anybody, 'cause she had no place better to go. She told me she had moved here from Johnson City and it was way worse than this. Said she grew up in a home where she had thirteen other siblings.

I didn't even know where Johnson City was, but I didn't care. I decided I would give her three hundred fifty thousand to leave that a-hole. She just had to divorce him first. Oh, I would pay for that as well. If she wouldn't do that then, no money for her! I made a note to call my attorney to schedule an appointment to go in. I needed to add a codicil to my will. I didn't want an entire new one, 'cause I'd already changed it three times.

Most of my friends think I'm just an old lady now and don't have the urge for wang, dang, slang. That's what the kids call it nowadays. Sometimes, I do. I just don't tell them. One thing I decided for sure; when I get this money business settled, I will call that Las Vegas Escort Service and find me one, something young and special.

Now, I knew from watching that TV show, "How the Lotto Changed my Life," everyone always buys a new house and car first. Not me. I didn't want to bring a whole lot of attention to myself. This house was just fine, it had worked for me all of these years; it would work for me now.

Another item on the list: I decided I would go over to my old neighborhood and leave ten thousand dollars in *The Commercial Appeal* on the porch of each house on my old street. I'll never forget the hard times growing up over there. We were so poor. I wasn't gonna leave my name, or a message. I'd just leave the money. If they didn't open that paper up and read it, then, oh well. I would leave it in the Wednesday paper. Most people buy the Wednesday paper. That's when the sales are listed and most poor folks are always looking for a sale.

I realized this was going to be fun! I guessed it's about fifteen to twenty houses on my old street. There are young couples who can barely make ends meet, single moms with kids, and a few older couples who are barely making it with their social security checks. Origill Street is just like it was back in my day, only people aren't as nice towards one another nowadays. Anyway, I would watch the news to see if the people on that street can keep a secret or if it will make the news. I also knew I better make sure to leave them all on the same day at the same time, cause people are so scandalous these days. If I left some on Tuesday and some on Wednesday, the Tuesday people might take the Wednesday people's paper off their porch.

So I made up my mind. I would deliver them all on the same day, Wednesday. I would just go straight to the newspaper company downtown and buy myself a stack of papers, just like the delivery people do. Let's see, I counted twenty houses. At two dollars per paper, that will total forty dollars. I would deliver them around four-thirty a.m. Most folks are still sleep then, and it's dark, so I shouldn't be seen. Now, who would I get to ride with me up to Nashville? Well, let's see, Loretta? No, she would tell. That girl tells all her business. Maybe Monica, she pretty much keeps to herself. No. She thinks I have a lot of money now. I would never get rid of her.

Then it occurred to me. I would call Limo Express. They would take me and bring me back. Now, could I trust them? I didn't want to end up missing from riding with some limo driver and never be found again. I thought a bit and decided what to do. I would have the limo service drop me off at the mall and return to pick me up in four hours. Then, I'd take a taxi from the mall to the place where I claimed my ticket. I'd get a different taxi back to the mall, and when my limo driver came back, I would be loaded with shopping bags. He would never know the difference. I'd be ready to go. I decided I had better make it five hours to be safe.

After that, I'd have more than enough money left to do some more great things for people I've come in contact with throughout the years. Let's see. What else did I want to do and who else did I want to bless now? I decided I would put two thousand dollars each in fifty envelopes. I'd buy fifty papers from them Muslim brothas. I'd explain that I just wanted them to pass out the papers to fifty people who would accept them. I'd have them say, "Today! Today! Free paper, free paper, my brotha; free paper, my sista."

Whoever takes the paper from them would end up with two thousand dollars. Most of them brothas seem like nice decent men, but people are so quick to just pass them by. Won't even hear a word they hafta say. Well, fifty people would have a chance to hear them at a red light. If they did, they wouldn't be sorry.

Now for Pastor Clarke and the church, I figured I would wait for the Christmas Eve service and give him two special envelopes, one for him, for being such a good shepherd, and one for the church. Some people talk trash about my pastor, but I think he's great. Like my mom used to say, "He can rightfully divide the word."

That's all that's required of him for me. I didn't know exactly what the church needed. The church is always clean and beautiful, plus it has a television broadcast. I decided I'd give him the money and he could do with it as he wished. I'd give the church five hundred thousand. Then I'd pay my tithes. Well, let's see. Ten percent would be about two hundred eighty-one thousand. I was sure the pastor would like that. He could figure out how to take what he needs for whatever. Now, did I want to let on that it's from me or just leave it anonymously?

I decided I would give those girls that my daughter hangs out with on Fridays a special treat, too. I would send them all on a trip out to the West Coast. My daughter tells me they get together the last Friday of each month to read and discuss a book. Something tells me it's a little bit more than that. I know my daughter. It took her a while to settle down. I love my son-in-law; it was a long time coming. That girl kept me worried all the time. She had a new guy every holiday or special occasion. Thanksgiving it was Nathaniel, Fourth of July it was Aaron, Christmas it was…what was his name? I thought he was a keeper, so cute and well mannered. Prentiss. At her sister's wedding, she had that clown named Eric. He was a partying fool. He was drinking champagne right out of the bottle, dancing and hunching all up on her butt, doing the dog or some kinda wild dance. Then a fight broke out between the two of them, and I had to have her sister's husband put him out. They almost got into a fistfight. That girl, that girl, she's always been wild. Used to leave home on Friday night and come back Monday evening after work. Would be tore down, but since she's been married to Myles she's slowed down a lot, and become a nice respectable wife. When she announced that she and Myles were getting married the whole family was happy.

I called Global Travel right away and had my girl set up a little trip for them." Hello, may I speak to Jellory?"

"One moment, please."

"This is Jellory. How may I help you?"

"This is Ms. G. How are you doing?"

"Just fine. And you?"

"Listen, Baby," I said to her, "I want to do something special for my daughter and about nine of her girlfriends. I want to send them on a trip out to the West Coast. I want the trip to be for a total of fourteen days. I want them to stay in the Los Angeles area for nine days and five days in Las Vegas. I want this round trip, first class. I want them flying on Delta Airlines. I love Delta, if you ain't on Delta you ain't on first class. I want them to stay in one of those nice upscale beachfront houses right on Malibu Beach, one where they can see the water as well as hear the waves, with enough room for the ten of them to be comfortable. I want limo service for them all the way. It should pick them up from the airport and take them whenever and wherever they might want to go. Then I want them to get a plane from there to Las Vegas, only this time, put them in one of the finest hotels that money can buy. None of that timeshare stuff. Make sure they have limo service there as well. All them girls think they're still young, but I got news for them. Things start to change once you get in your fifties, and I believe most of them are fifty- something. Okay, Jellory? Yeah, let me know what you come up with, Baby."

"Um, how much time do I have to get this all together, Ms. G?

"Well, I figure they will want to travel sometime next year. I want to give it to them as a Christmas present."

"Okay, I'll be back in touch. Thanks Ms. G."

"No. Thank *you*, Baby."

I went back to my list. What and who else did I have on here? Okay, my nephews. Well, let's see, there are two musicians in the family, one preacher and three struggling baby daddies. Those boys are something else. All so handsome though. I prayed for girls, didn't want no boys. Now, the two musicians. I knew they were age twenty-five and thirty. I decided I'd give the twenty-five-year-old, twenty-five thousand towards his music career and the thirty-year-old, thirty thousand. That preaching nephew was thirty-five, and boy could he preach. He had his own congregation now. I'd donate thirty-five thousand to his church ministry. And those three baby daddies, I'd give each one of them thirty thousand, too. However, I would place half of their money, fifteen thousand, in a trust for their kids. Once the kid reached twenty-five years of age, they could have their money. That seemed fair and safe.

Well, I didn't have to worry about setting up any trust for my girls and their kids. I did that a long time ago. Now I could just add money to it. I had long since paid for my own grave plot, headstone, casket, funeral and all. I decided I'd invest a small amount in a few more shares of stock from FedEx, Google, and AT&T. Someone mentioned lithium batteries was a good investment. Nowadays they are using batteries for everything, cars, cell phones, and all kinds of devices. I would check into that too. And I really liked that new e-book stuff. Seemed like every day I was hearing about so many different kinds of electronic devices.

Now my university, I would hafta give them something. Good old T. S. U. I decided to donate two hundred fifty thousand. That would help someone out. I planned to help a few of my noisy friends, like Vanessa, Troy, and Russell. I would just send them a cashier's check by FedEx and a small note that will say, "Enjoy. From your friend to the end. I'm having a ball. See y'all!"

I never knew it could be so much fun giving away money and spending it without checking and rechecking my checkbook. I lost thirty percent because I wanted it all at one time instead of over the years, and I still had more than enough for me to share. Hell, who knows how long you have left on this earth. It's called one day at a time for me. Now I knew how the wealthy felt, and it felt pretty damn good.

I read back over my list. I had done something for everybody on my list now except myself. I'd been saving all of my life and carefully watching what I spent; now it was time to splurge.

I still hadn't told anyone outright that I'd won the lotto yet. No need in telling them now and spoiling all of my fun. I'd run out of places to put my yard money. I had no more room in the backyard or either side of the house. So the next best thing, I thought, was to get me a greenhouse built in the back just like I like it. I'd wanted one for so long and now I was going to get it.

After two weeks, I still hadn't heard from my little travel agent girl. I wondered if she'd forgotten me, but probably not. I knew she's pretty thorough and I had given her quite a tall order. I figured it just takes time. I knew them girls would meet the next month and I wanted my baby to take the present out to them when she went. Next week was Thanksgiving and the week after that we would run into December. I decided to give her until the Saturday after Thanksgiving. If I hadn't heard from her by then, I'd give her a call to see how my request is coming along.

Thanksgiving was gonna be at my sister's house. I sure hated driving that 240 East Interstate. They are always working on the road. But it only took an hour and a half to get there, and Thanksgiving comes only once a year, so I would just do it.

Her house was large enough for whoever wants to stay over. She loved company. I remember when she moved way out there, that husband of hers was so picky. He didn't want the kids to run in or outside the house, couldn't stand my sister's bird. Can't much blame him, though. That damn bird was loud, some kind of parrot. I think it was called a macaw. What was his name? Paco. That damn bird talked more than a radio. Whenever the telephone rang, he'd say, "Phone ringing. Phone ringing. Phone ringing," and when the doorbell rang, he'd say, "Get the door. Get the door. Get the door."

Her husband, we called him Big Country, he worried about people sitting on the couch, where they ate, and if they got too loud. She told me, he don't hear well, so I'm trying to figure out, if that's the case, why should noise bother him? He was so controlling, and he'd been that way for years. My brother-in-law was special. My sister used to be stressed out all the time. He controlled the whole house, from the kitchen to the back yard, and everything in between. He's ten years older than her, and now that he'd gotten older and so slow, it didn't matter to him anymore. But he still had to have control of the remote whenever everyone was over. We all knew, so we just let him. Just about every room had a big screen TV now. That made him happy and everyone else too. That made him feel like he was still in control. They had a lake out back where all the grandkids loved to come out to fish and play. There was enough land for him and his brothers to go out during the winter and hunt for deer. He loved to go to the woods. When Thanksgiving came around, he and his five brothers, and other in-laws would all get together. We wouldn't see them anymore until dinnertime.

I said if she likes it, then I love it. Me, I could never do it. I'd be on the next episode of *Snapped*. I couldn't have kept my mouth shut. I'd hafta speak my mind.

That's why when my man died, I said never, ever, again. Now, he was good to me. He always did things to make me happy. When I would ask him what he wanted to do, he would always say, "Whatever you want to do." I could ask him what he wanted for dinner and he'd say, "Whatever you feel like cooking." He paid all of the bills and gave me money every month, even though I had my own. We went everywhere together, to the casino, the church, out of town, on cruises, Las Vegas. Even went to Paris and Hawaii. We had many days of parties with other couples. We played cards, had barbecue cookouts, and he never missed a week of bringing me fresh flowers.

I still missed him, even though it had been some years since he passed away. I knew I would never find another man like him. So I have just been enjoying my life alone. Sometimes, I thought it would be nice to have a companion to do things with in my old age. Then, I would snap out of it and come to my senses, thinking about some of the horror stories I'd heard from my sister and a few of my other girlfriends.

While the guys were out hunting, the four of us sisters had time to bond. I wanted to tell them so bad that I'd won the lottery, but I knew if I did, the whole family would go crazy and I would suddenly become everyone's favorite aunt, sister, cousin, and friend. I decided I'd just keep it to myself for now.

I had another thought: When I got home, I'd remember to put down on my "Things to do" list to add twenty thousand to my casino purse.

EVA

William was still trying everything he could to satisfy and keep me happy. I was so tired of it. It was becoming quite aggravating, but I didn't let him know. I just acted as if everything was okay. Fake it until you make it! That's what I'd been doing lately and spending a little too much time eating all the wrong things. Like three and four times a week at the butcher shop, Texas De Brazil for lunch, ordering special cupcakes, chocolate-covered strawberries, and pies from this young lady at church who's trying to make money for her college education. She is really good and someone is going to come along and recognize her soon. Before you know it, she will have her own bakery or become a well-known chef. She's that good. I think I had gained an extra fifteen pounds since I'd been purchasing all this sweet stuff from her.

My friend Jessica called again and talked to me about her book club. It's full right now, but she thinks it would really help me. She wanted to put my name in when a space does come open. I just shook my head." I don't want to be hanging out with a bunch of boring ass women talking about a book."

"I bet you would. I think it would be just the thing for you."

"You think that will help me get out of this slump I'm in?"

"Yes, ma'am. I'm gonna put your name down."

In September, William told me that he'd done some research on penile implants." Not a lot of down time and the doctor thought it would work for us."

I told him that if that would make him happy then I was all for it. I would call Jessica and ask in a round about way about it. She'd dated a guy who'd had the procedure and he was older than William.

William called me from work on a Friday evening and said, "Hey, Baby. Get up, get dressed, and be ready to go when I get home. Tonight, I'm taking you out on the town."

"What's the occasion? You got a promotion?"

He chuckled, "It's a surprise. No kids. Call your niece and see if she could come over for three to four hours. Make sure you tell her Uncle Willis paying. I know that will get her over here."

What could be going on? He sounded so happy. Later, when I heard Will coming up the steps, I was just about ready. I had a hard time deciding what to wear, my new Giorgio Armani pantsuit or the Dana Buchman dress. These were two of the outfits I bought when we went to the West Coast for our anniversary. Just as I had decided, and was putting on my pants, Will walked into my closet. I was sitting at my dressing table and he was smiling from ear to ear. He had a dozen beautiful peach and yellow roses. I gave him a smack on the lips and said, "Thank you, Baby."

"You look great, Baby," he said. "We are going to Grill 83 tonight. We have two things to celebrate. Number one, you are looking at the new Captain on Delta Airlines. No more worrying about looking for the best air fares; we got buddy passes. And number two, my doctor called and scheduled a date for my surgery. I am going to get that penile implant, Baby! Then I will be able to satisfy you completely. Anytime. Any day. Any way."

I was almost afraid to hope that God had answered my prayers. William's surgery was scheduled for the end of October at Vanderbilt Medical Center. I planned to be right there with my man, and I was keeping my fingers crossed this would be the solution to our problem.

I was not really a cheater. My momma didn't raise me that way. From my upbringing in the church, it's called sinning, and I knew it. I'd asked God, and I felt he'd forgiven me.

William came through his surgical procedure just fine. Dr. Evans said he would need to rest for six to eight weeks, and no hanky-panky before then. He said William should be good to go afterwards, and that he was sure I'd be pleased. He left some pamphlets for me at the nurse's station along with aftercare instructions.

"Give me a call if you need anything," he said.

"Thanks Doctor Evans. I hope you're right."

"I promise you little lady, you'll be happy."

We finally got the okay to leave the hospital around six p.m. We've been there since five a.m. I was tired. My poor baby, he was hurting and moaning pretty bad as I was pushing him in the wheelchair toward the exit. He was so drugged up. I figured I would take him home first and then shoot over to Walgreen's and pick up his prescription. He had two, morphine for pain and some kind of antibiotic. That pain medicine would keep him knocked out for a while. I was glad we have a bedroom down stairs as well as up. He couldn't possibly have made it up anyone's stairs right now. I helped William in and out of the car. When we got home, I helped him into his pajamas, got the pillows and cover just right on the bed, and put the remote, his cell phone, house phone, laptop, and phone charger all on the nightstand at his reach, just in case he felt up to working or reading or looking or talking or whatever.

As I was leaving for Walgreen's, I looked back at my husband and the Bobby Caldwell song, *What We Won't Do For Love,* ran through my head, "I guess you wondering where I've been. I searched to find a love within. I came back to let you know, got a thing for you and I can't let go."

My husband was such a fine, handsome man, and maybe, just maybe, this would do the trick. I picked up the medicine, then drove over to my big sis's house and got the kids. I told them to be quiet going in the house 'cause Daddy wasn't feeling well.

Evan Laire' looked worried. "Momma, what's wrong with Daddy? He didn't seem sick to me last night."

"Oh, he's okay. He just had to get a little procedure done at the doctor. He's gonna be fine in a few days."

"Can I go see him, Momma?"

"You can go in his room later. He's resting right now."

When I got back, he was asleep. I gave William a little bell, also. I probably wouldn't hear him if he just tried to call me, but the bell was so damn loud, I'd hear that. I went up to our bedroom upstairs to relax a bit. When I'd gotten myself settled, I took out that pamphlet to read what was in store for me.

That Sunday the kids and I went to church without Will. He was walking around a little bit, but still healing. I had read the pamphlet, and I was becoming more optimistic. I thought once we learned how to work that thing, it might be just fine.

Days and weeks went by pretty fast and when William had two weeks time in from the procedure, he started coming around. He talked on the phone, stayed on the computer, and was running me like a maid. He wore me out with that bell I gave him. He said once he returned back to work, it would be a while before he'd have any time off because of his new position, so he wanted to take me on a quiet trip, just us two.

He told me while we were chitchatting that he loved me so much and would do anything to keep me happy. He told me that he thanked God every day for blessing him with such a good wife and that I meant the world to him.

"I appreciate how you've been there for me, and for being such a good, god-fearing, faithful wife. I just want to show you how much I appreciate you. I've been checking places online and I've found us a nice bed and breakfast place up in Gatlinburg. I think it will be just what we need to get back on track." Then he grabbed me and kissed me long and hard. "I love you, Baby."

BECKY

It was fall now and everyone seemed so down. We had lost a true friend and member of our book club and we were all tripping about finding a replacement. I asked everyone to get here an hour early at the next meeting so we can discuss business before we got into our routine.

I was almost to exit 64. Five minutes and I would be there. I could see Ms. Phyllis was there, early as usual. We could always count on Phyllis. I was thinking maybe we should make Ms. Phyllis a member. I didn't know if she can afford to be in, but I thought about putting her name in the hat, maybe.

"Hey, girl, how are you doing?" I asked her.

"Just fine, Beck. I got everything ready and it's time to paaaaaarty!"

"Tonight may be a little different, Phyllis. Everyone's kinda sad that Rose is gone. Well, most of us, except Faye and Foy. Those sistas don't give a damn about nobody but themselves. Tonight we have to try and figure out who will take her place, so it might be pretty laid back. I'm going upstairs to sit in the lounge area where I can see everyone pull in before it gets dark. I know Faye and Foy will be last. They're always last. Oh! Here comes Renee in her bad ass red Porsche. Her husband got that for her last year on Mother's Day."

We all had our own personal reasons for being in the book club, but we rarely openly discussed them amongst each other. If it wasn't for Viagra and Cialis, a lot of these old dogs we're married to wouldn't have been kicking it as long as they have. Who ever made that shit has a can of good old-fashioned whoop ass coming to them.

Every member had a story. Faye got caught up with some man who used to detail her Corvette, and it took some convincing to get her husband to calm down. After that, strictly book club all the way. Yolanda, she was the shit talker in the group. Always coming up with something funny to say, or giving someone a funny name. Liked to call Rose, Risky Rose, and Jernethia, Jamming J, 'cause there ain't an old school song that she don't know all the words to.

Renee was so nervous, always worrying that we were gonna get caught and our secret would get out. Every time she'd get to the club, she would say, "Hurry up girls. Let's get started. I don't want to be too late getting home."

She thought her old man had some kind of tracking device on her car and cell phone. Had to tell her to chill out every time, but after her first glass of Chardonnay she's on.

Now Foy, that was a partying ass girl. She would come in the door talking loud, heading straight to the bar, dancing all the way. She loved her some Michael Jackson. If you put on *Thriller*, she started cutting up! She loved to hook up with David. He's rough and wild. The two of them get buck wild, dancing all down to the floor. He'll be smacking her butt, and she'll be smacking his. He's always been the one to take the party to another level.

And there was Valerie. She walked in saying, "Where da party at! If you ain't here to party, take your old ass home. I came to party all night long, and I am looking for my favorite glass of Patron."

She loved to wear some kind of top with her boobs hanging out, always had her hair braided. She said she don't like combing her hair; it always looked good.

There went Foy, upstairs with that wild man David, and he was grinning all the way, treating her like she was Michael Jackson. Now Renee, she had gained quite a bit of weight, and lately, she seemed a little self-conscious. She always acted so shy. Her favorite was Jonathan. I saw her fix a glass of wine and head for the herbal tray. Then they disappeared down to the lower level where the Jacuzzi was. I knew I wouldn't see her any more until time to go. I knew Jessica would have liked to own Neville. He was known for giving a good massage.

Me, I liked Basil and Lincoln. They had a way of using their tongue like no one I've ever known in my entire fifty-three years of life. It was always a party. The book club was what every girl needed to keep a happy, happy marriage. You know, "Happy Wife, Happy Life."

Earlier, Jernethia had passed out the forms I made for each of us to write down the name of the person they want to join our book club. Each of us was to leave it in the box on the table as she entered the house. Jessica had someone in mind that's younger than us, I believe in her thirties, but she thought she would make a great fit. Eva was her name. Well, we'll see who we come up with.

MABEL

At 10 a.m. I called. "Hello, Mr. Cavanaugh, this is Mabel Sutton. I was in on Friday and you gave me the candy apple red CTS for me and my mother to try out over the weekend. Yeah. Well, she loves it! Can you get the paperwork together and call me when it's ready, and I'll bring my mom in to sign?"

"Sure thing. So…she loved it?"

"Yes. Yes, she did."

"Give me about, oh let's say…hour and a half. After that you ladies can come over anytime."

"Whew," I thought. "Let me call mom so she can get ready. She isn't going out without looking her best."

When I got to her house at eleven a.m., she had on a tan with red trimmed St. John knit suit, this time with red accessories and red bag. Looking good. God, I hope I can look as good as she does when I get her age. That is, if I'm blessed to live that long. I must say, my momma had it going on; petite, nice figure, only about a hundred twenty-five pounds, pretty hair, and speaks well with only having a sixth grade education.

It took us a little longer than thirty minutes to get there. It looked like something was going on. The highway traffic was kinda backed-up. Thought it was an accident, but, no; it was some kind of construction going on. They were always working on this highway. You see, this is a military town. They have to keep things right for our soldiers. They are the ones who keep this town alive. That's how this town makes their money. If the Army pulled out of here, this town would go broke. We got there at noon. Mr. Cavanaugh met us before we could get out of the car. He was being so polite and kind. He was kinda cute in his own strange way, freckles and red hair, but dressed just as sharp as any black man could. I noticed that he chewed. I saw that tobacco hump in his jaw. Ugh.

"Ms. Luizer, so nice to meet you. I've heard a lot about you. Can I get you anything to drink, coffee or a soda or water?"

"No," she smiled back at him, "The old lady is just fine."

With that, he led us straight to the office where they write up all the paperwork. His office, of course, was very plush. It had leather seats, a mahogany desk, and pictures of himself and two older men.

The first thing he said was, "So how do you like the car?"

"It's a mighty fine car, sir," momma said, still saying "Sir," when she was old enough to be his momma. No, grandmomma. No, great grandmomma.

Then he changed tactics.

"Now, Ms. Luizer, I told your daughter that we would take your old Cadillac as a trade and no money down, but we got a big problem. That old Cadillac of yours is just about no good. You got sixty-five thousand miles on it and a couple of dents on the passenger side, as well as quite a few scratches in the interior. So I won't be able to make you the trade-in deal I discussed with your daughter, which was, I believe I told her, ten-thousand. But I can give you two thousand for it."

"How is that possible?" she said, "I only owe a few more payments and the car is only three years old. You're telling me that's all it's worth?"

"Yes, ma'am."

"Well, what would that make my monthly payment be?"

"Right now you pay four hundred dollars per month, but this fine car that you're in now will run you about a thousand."

"You must be kidding, sir."

"No, ma'am. With your trade in and no money down, that's the best I can do for you."

I thought, "He must be out of his mind; my momma ain't going for that. I should've known it was too good to be true."

She looked at him and said, "No. No. I know you wouldn't try to use that Red Zone special on an old lady, now would you, Baby?"

"Excuse me, what do you mean? I don't know what you're referring to."

"With the Red Zone special, people put Cadillacs either in the layaway, have balloon payments or they pay every couple of weeks instead of monthly, to drive a car they can't really afford."

What he didn't know, and I didn't know, was that Ms. Luizer, my momma, used to work for and help raised his father, the owner of Horlew Cadillac. She also took care of his grandfather as well. He didn't expect this, didn't expect her to be as sharp as she was.

Momma told him, "Go get your daddy, or get him on the phone right now. Tell him Ms. Luizer is down here in his car store and that you're trying to sell me a car at the Red Zone special. You give that silliness to other folks who don't know no better, but not to Ms. Luizer. You think I'm old, slow, and don't know any better, and that my daughter was just trying to take me for a ride.

"Well, I am going for a ride, and it's going to be in that red car that I just came in, for the price and car note that I currently pay. Get your daddy!"

"Excuse me, I'll be right back."

When Joel Cavanaugh returned, Mr. Jack Cavanaugh, CEO and owner of Horlew Cadillac, himself stepped in. He came over and gave my mom a hug."Hey, Momma Luzier. So glad to see you."

"Boy, where you been? You done got so fat. How old are you now? You getting a little grey around the sides, too. I remember when you were born with that little red hair standing straight up on top of your head.

"I never met your baby boy before. He's pretty sharp, but he's still got a lot to learn. You need to teach him to check the background of his customers before he starts to try and give them that Red Zone special. He needs to know it don't apply to everyone, like me, you know what I mean?

"Say, did you meet my baby, Mabel? She's just as spoiled as can be. I had her around the time you were going off to college, and after her, that was the end of my working days. Elvis wouldn't let me work for nobody no more after she came. I spent a lot of days working over there in Plantation Estates. I was getting a little bit older when I had her.

"Well, anyway... let me stop talking about nothing and get to talking about that fine car he sent my baby home in. I want to make it mine. Your baby sent my Mabel home with this new Cadillac for me to try out, and I just love it. However, he's telling me it's going to cost me a thousand dollars a month. I can't…I won't pay that kind of money. I need you to fix this. Now don't blame him; I know he was just trying to do his job and my baby didn't know to tell him who I was, either."

"Don't you worry, Momma Luizer. Just give me a minute and I'll be right back."

Jack and Joel stepped outside the door and I heard his father raise his voice and say, "Don't ever forget to look on the exempt list and the archive file before you start talking a sale."

Joel came back in just as red in the face as he was in his hair. "I am sorry, Ms. Luizer. I apologize for the inconvenience. Everything is all set. Can you give me about forty-five minutes to get the car washed, tank filled, and all the paperwork in order?"

By one-thirty p.m. my momma was signing paperwork and, by two-fifteen, we were on the road in our new car. "I'm glad we got that over, Momma," I said, "Are you tired?"

"Yes Baby. I'm a little tired, and I guess we need to stop somewhere for lunch. Then you can take the old lady home. Next week I want you to take me over to Paris Landing. I need to see my attorney. I got some important business to take care of with him."

"Okay, Momma, just let me know when you're ready and I'll be there."

"I'm gonna call the law office first thing tomorrow and make an appointment. You go on and enjoy the car for a few days, and figure out how to work some more of those fancy bells and whistles before I ride again. You know, Mabel, I'm liking this car. If your daddy was still alive he would approve of it, too."

As I was backing out of Momma's driveway in her new bad-ass car, I was thinking about what she said to that man. Did she actually work as a maid? She'd never mentioned anything about working at no Plantation Estates. And what in the hell was the Red Zone Special? My momma had some secrets. I needed to start listening a little closer to what Momma had to say when we're together. I could tell something else was on her mind, but I just couldn't put my finger on it. For now, I'd keep watching. It had been a long day, and I was ready to go home to chill.

Wow, guess I was tired; that glass of wine put me straight to sleep. I didn't even hear the phone ring. I had a message from my girlfriend Renee. She wanted to know if everything worked out at Horlew and if we really, really had that bad-ass car. I smiled. That girl's so damn nosy. I would call her later. I didn't want to be bothered tonight.

I woke up at nine, got my shower, and headed out around eleven. I can have fun all by myself, don't hafta have someone with me all the time. I like me. No, I love me. I decided I'd ride out to West Town Mall to see what was new at Caché and look for a Coach purse, preferably red. That would give me some riding time to get more of a feel for the car. I'd probably run into a little lunch traffic, but that's okay. I ain't got nothin' but time.

I pulled right into the mall, and parked up front in the handicapped parking area. People always look at me as if to say, "She don't look handicapped." This is just one of the perks of having an eighty-year-old momma that's got it going on. She said she's too old to be walking long distances.

Now let's see now, I've got Momma's and my seat programmed, satellite radio stations set, navigation system set, and all of me and Momma's favorite places programmed. Haven't figured out how to set my cell phone with the Bluetooth yet , and I might have to go back up to Horlew so they can go over changing hard top to rag top. I have no idea how to work that yet. Most all the features in this car are touch screen, just like my cell phone. Navigation system works well. It said, "Take slight right on 24 West. Then merge to I-65 North. Estimated time of arrival 9:15."

As I drove home I thought, "Seems like Momma would've called me on this car phone today, but I haven't heard a word from her. I love this car. It's great. I'll run my bathwater, then call Momma."

I was so glad my pet is a feline. I would've been in serious trouble if I'd had a dog. I'd been gone way too long, and the house would be smelling by now. That's why I love Livey. The last place I lived, my neighbor had the most beautiful cat I'd ever seen in my life. I asked her what kind it was, and she said it was a Himalayan. She gave me a number for a lady that breeds them. That was the only time I'd ever been to Paris, Tennessee. Ms. Livey cost me eight hundred dollars. She's eight years old now and we know each other pretty well. She can always tell when it's time for my book club meeting, purrs…all day. We're just too old pussies, living like queens.

I picked up the phone, "Hey, Momma, how you doing?"

"Oh, I'll say just fine. I was thinking about you. Good to check on your old momma, 'cause I could be dead in the morning."

"Oh, Momma, stop saying that. You gonna be around for a long time. Did you decide when you want to go over to Paris?"

"Yes, I called and my appointment is next Wednesday at two p.m."

"Okay, Momma. Well, I just wanted to call and check on you and see if you need anything. I drove the car out to West Town Mall and it rides good. I've learned how to work a few more things."

"I like that. That's good news."

"I'm gonna take my soak now, Momma. Goodnight."

As I was in the tub soaking I thought, "One week from today, wonder who, what, or why we're really going to Paris. Wonder what kind of secret Momma has there."

KEITH

My secretary stuck her head around my door just as she headed out to lunch. "You have a Ms. Luizer Sutton scheduled for two p.m., remember." Since I was semi-retired, I only worked a couple of days a week, and she had made the appointment for me when I was out.

"Who? Ms. Luizer Sutton?"

"Yes, sir."

"I haven't seen her in years."

"I couldn't find her in our current files, but I found her in the archives. Looks like you did a divorce for her ages ago."

That lady was one of my first clients when I started practicing law. She told me that she randomly picked me out of the telephone book. Said she liked the sound of my name, Attorney Keith Shainberg.

I met my wife, Selina, while I was in law school. She was so supportive throughout my seven years of schooling. She was the most beautiful girl I'd ever seen. I remember that she worked in the law library office as a secretary. I wondered how this woman…where this woman came from. You don't see too many Chinese people around Tennessee. I took her home to meet my mom and dad. They were friendly, but didn't have too much to say. They always supported me in whatever I did and when I announced to them that I wanted to marry her, my mom only asked that I wait until I finished law school. I did that for her.

Selina was so sweet and she was made up just like a little doll. We had a routine dinner every Friday night. She'd always asked me how my day was, and she was a great listener, too. I knew she was a keeper and that she would take care of me. We got married after five years of dating. I immediately joined the law firm and worked with my dad.

Our first house was very small. My dad bought it as a wedding present for us. Selina always kept it neat and clean. We always made time for each other, and every Friday was still our special day. I would bring home fresh flowers, take her out for a candlelight dinner, and afterwards, we would come home and play soft music. She'd put on something extra sexy. I always took my time with her, and I was always very gentle. Our bed was the biggest piece of furniture we owned. It was given to me by my grandmother when she passed away. It was a mahogany feather bed with the four tall posts. She would try and get a little feisty on some of our Friday nights of fun and swing around the bedpost like a stripper would do. I was a happy man, and I thought one day we'd have a little person running around here. We didn't have a lot of money, but life was good, and we made the best with what we had. I thought she was happy, too, and had the same wishes as me, but I found out differently.

After I had been working at the law office with my father for about a year, things began to change between us. I was making a pretty decent living now. We could afford to have a child or two. We purchased a large home on Sunrise Drive. It was beautiful and had enough room for a houseful of children if we wanted them.

Selina would come by the office to have lunch with me everyday, something we used not to be able to do. I worked longer hours, but I always made time for her. She never had to work, even when we lived on a small budget. With the money I was making now, she could have just about anything she wanted. I gave her an unlimited American Express card to use as she pleased. I made sure that once a year she could go to Hawaii to spend two weeks or more with her mother and visit family and friends.

She didn't have very many friends of her own in town here. I tried to get her to join several different groups around town, introduced her to other wives of fellow attorneys, but she just wasn't interested in making any friends. I always tried to make her happy, but I sensed something was missing between us.

Something was missing for me, too. I longed for a child in our lives. I finally convinced her to seek medical help. She got tired of me complaining and pleading with her so much that she finally made an appointment to see a doctor. They ran several tests on her, and the results were that Selina couldn't have children. We tried everything, artificial insemination, checking the timing when she ovulated, this way, that way. Everything except adoption. I was totally against that because I was afraid of what kind of child we might get. I've seen a few juvenile court cases where the kids weren't so nice. Some of those kids were truly shepherds for the devil.

So I tried to make her, and myself, happy in other ways. I gave her more money, fabulous dinners, special jewelry, and trips to exotic places. Nothing seemed to work. She seemed to have turned distant and cold, and I didn't know what had happened or why she changed.

When little Ms. Luizer Sutton came to my office for a divorce, I had never given any other woman a second look, but she was beautiful. I'd never handled a divorce case before. She told me she'd been married for fifteen years and that her husband was very abusive. Not so much physically, but mentally. He always talked down to her, kept her away from the things she loved, and never gave her a penny for herself. She wasn't allowed to communicate with her family or friends. Never allowed to have any say so on anything. She just didn't want to live like that any longer. She was afraid of him. He was a military man, and he controlled everything, from what she wore to the food she ate. He only allowed certain furniture in the house, and demanded that she wash the towels daily. If he got home and they weren't clean and back in their proper place, he'd make her hold out her hands, front side up, and he'd slap them with a branch. Ms. Sutton said she was tired, and had stayed with him this long only because she had nowhere else to go.

She explained that she finally had enough money to pay for her divorce and start over on her own. Her husband didn't know about the money and house left by her father, or he would've controlled that too. Her mother had long passed away and she was the only child. She said her mind was made up and she was ready to get it over with. He had promised to do something bad to her father if she tried to leave. So she stayed, but now that her father was gone, he could no longer hold that over her head.

Now I understood why she didn't have the divorce handled by an attorney in Clarksville. That explained why she drove to Paris. She was such a beautiful young woman. She had the biggest sexy brown eyes that I'd ever seen, and long black wavy hair. She looked like a little doll. I'd never met a Black woman who was so attractive to me. She even sounded sexy over the phone.

When I heard her voice in my head I was thinking, "I wonder what it would be like to make love to her," but I remained professional.

It took a total of one year to get that divorce finalized. When we served papers on her spouse, he went crazy. He contested the divorce and tried to say she had committed adultery and had a drinking problem. He had no proof of anything. She was awarded alimony and also half of his military retirement. She also received half of the sale of land that he owned that she never knew about, and half of the money he'd stashed in another bank account in Memphis. She paid me, thanked me, and we parted ways.

Then one day about a year later, I was going out to have some quiet time by myself out on the boat at Paris Landing. I needed to get away from all the paperwork at the office. I bought that boat for me and my wife, but she didn't seem interested in spending any time there with me. My wife was away on her yearly visit to Hawaii. My boat was where I could always find peace. It was a calming place for me.

I played my guitar and harmonica for a while, took a nap, and just relaxed and listened to all of the sounds from the lake. I looked at my watch and was surprised I'd been there for at least half the day. I thought that I'd better head on home.

As I gathered my guitar and things, I could see this lady from a distance. She had on this long peach and brown floral printed dress that showed off her every curve and her hair was blowing in the wind. She was a petite little thing, just sitting under a tree, reading out on the lawn behind the little hotel at the water's edge. I gathered my glasses and guitar and headed near her to get a closer look. When I did, I saw it was Ms. Luizer, that same young woman whom I helped get free from her marriage.

I said, "Well, well, well. If it isn't Ms. Luizer Sutton! How have you been, married again? "

"No. No way. I have friends now and I can come and go as I please."

"Well, let me buy you lunch, if you don't have anything planned right now."

We went to the Blue Plate Café. She said, "I live in my dad's old house in Clarksville now, but I like coming here. It's so peaceful. It takes me exactly two hours to get here, but it's worth the drive. I usually spend the night at the Paris Landing State Park Inn for a day or two then head home."

We talked about everything, the weather, the military guys in Fort Campbell, Kentucky, my wife, her ex-husband, children, people, and some of my weird court cases. We laughed as if we were old friends. Then something happened, and I kissed her. Never kissed another woman since my wife and I got married. It felt good; it felt right. She felt something and so did I.

She invited me up to her room and one thing led to another. I forgot how good it felt to be held and kissed. I saw that I could still give as well as receive pleasure. Afterwards, we lay there in each other's arms listening to the sounds of the water from Paris Landing. Finally I had to pull away and head home." Luizer, this has meant so much to me. Promise me you'll keep in touch."

She said that she would.

My wife came back from Hawaii and it was just as before, still, lifeless and dull. No more Friday night romantic evenings. She would cook dinner and off to her room she'd go. Two months passed by, and one day I came in and I had a message from Ms. Luizer Sutton. My heart started to beat fast. I called her right away. She told me she would be in Paris on next Thursday and asked if I could meet her at the same place we met last time. I met her in the same room. All the same things went on. This soon became a regular thing for us. For the next six months, once a week, Luizer and I met in room 201.

Then, she just disappeared. I gave it a month and no word. I couldn't take it any longer, so I pulled her file and dialed the number we had listed for her. That number had been disconnected. I had no idea how to find her in Clarksville, and I didn't dare go snooping around and asking questions. People get hurt like that. She never called again.

Now, all these years later, she was coming to my office to see me. I really wondered what happened. I never knew what I did wrong, or didn't do. Maybe this was my chance to find out.

She had aged, but to me she was just as beautiful as she had been fifty years ago.

"I need to have a will made as well as a power of attorney, living will, and power of attorney for healthcare. I also have some income property that I want to have my daughter's name added to the title. How long do you think it will take to prepare all the paperwork?"

"I have a form that you'll need to fill out for me. It should give me all the information I'll need. Then my secretary can get started, and it should be ready in a week. Can you come back then?

"Sure, I can have my daughter bring me back. Well, I better check with her first."

"So you have a daughter now?"

"Yes, I brought her with me. Let me have her come in. She's out in the car. I would like you to meet her. Let me call her on this cell phone. She loves to keep me updated with all the new technology."

Her daughter was in the room within minutes. Luizer said, "Attorney Shainberg, meet my daughter, Mabel Sutton. This is my baby. She's 40 years old, but she's still my baby. She doesn't like me to call her my baby, but she is and she's all I got. I'm getting older now and I want to make sure she won't have any financial problems if anything happens to me."

When I saw her, my mouth flew open. I broke out in a sweat. She had features the same size and shape as mine, and she had wavy hair like her mother's, except it was the same auburn color as mine. She also didn't look like she really belonged to Luizer, but more like, like…could it really be? She looked like me. How…why? She never called me, never asked for a dime. She could see it in my flushed face. That girl staring me in my face was like me looking in a mirror. She was…she was my daughter! I didn't need to ask. I could see it for myself. She extended out her hand and said, "Nice to meet you, Mr. Shainberg. Do you need me for anything else, momma? Do I need to sign anything?"

"No, Honey, not right now. But can you bring me back on next Thursday? Attorney Shainberg will have my paperwork ready by then."

"Sure, Momma, I have one more week off before I go back to work. "

"Well, then, I'll let ya'll finish up. I'm gonna go back out to the car and wait for you. I've just about figured out how to work the convertible top on the car."

When she walked out, I said, "Why didn't you tell me? You knew how to find me. I would've helped you, helped her. Why?"

She told me the whole story. "When we were together, it was shortly after I'd divorced my husband. He tried to convince me to come back to him and I almost did. One night I went out with him, and he got pretty drunk and forced himself on me. On that one night, Mabel was conceived, or so we thought. I had a really rough pregnancy, and even though our divorce was final, he saw me through the pregnancy. He's taken care of Mabel all of her life, and he's the only father she's ever known. She has no idea that her so-called father and I were divorced. I've kept quite a few secrets from her. He stayed on tours—Germany, Korea, Egypt—and he provided a very generous allotment for the both of us. He was always there for her. He never forgot her birthdays, Christmas, accomplishments at school, nothing or anything that had to do with her. When Mabel was born with such fair skin and those freckles, I knew she was yours. I thought for sure he would say it wasn't his child, but he never thought twice. His grandmother was white. He just assumed she got it from his side of the family. I knew it was your child from the very start, and I've lived with this secret for forty years. At my age now, what can I say?"

She paused and touched my arm, "I wanted to call you so many times to tell you, but something always made me change my mind. I didn't want to disrupt your family life, your marriage. I knew we could never be together, no such thing as a white man marrying a black woman back then, especially in Tennessee. So I kept it a secret. Keith, I'm eighty years old now and to be free I have to tell you. I don't want to leave this earth without telling someone my secret. I know that someone should be you."

"Oh, Luizer, I would've been so proud to have been her father, your husband, boyfriend. Whatever. We could've worked it out."

"Hush now, Keith. Don't say that."

"I was hurt when I couldn't find you. I thought you felt something for me, too, Luizer. How could you just walk away and never look back on what we had?"

"I'm sorry, but I knew it would've never worked. It would've just been trouble. Please, Keith, we're too old now and too much time has gone by. Let's just leave it our secret."

"I never had any children with my wife and I always longed to be a father, wanted to bring at least one child on this earth before I died. I guess my wish did come true. I just didn't know about it."

"You know she's a Court Reporter down in Davidson County? She loves working in the legal field, too."

Never in a million years would I have known that we conceived a child.

As Luizer sat there filling out the form I asked her, "Does any one else know?"

"Yes, only one person, my dear friend, Bud. He lives down in Woodstock. We grew up in the country together. We played together as kids, which you didn't see often back in those days. Blacks and whites went to separate schools, but we lived about a mile from each other and our parents let us play together. We are still friends to this day. That's one of the reasons I'm here. He recently lost his one and only love. She wouldn't marry him and kept their relationship a secret until she died. So he's been after me to come see you and tell you the truth. Before it's too late."

"Luizer, you know that's true. I recently lost a loved one, my brother. He lived down in Memphis, actually my half brother, Henry Charles."

She shook her head. "I knew him! He was the real estate attorney at the closing when I purchased a house I bought some years ago as an investment over in Eads. I am so sorry, Keith. Was he married?"

"Yes, and he had a special friend, too. She meant everything to him."

"Yes, tomorrow is not promised."

"I know it's too late to tell Mabel who I really am, but I'd like to get to know her. And Luizer, my life has changed, too. My wife passed on some years back. I would like to spend time with you as well as Mabel."

"I don't know, Keith. I'll try, but I can't make any promises."

SARA

I sure had a good time out at my sister's. Just had to try and keep a straight face about my secret. I kept having hot flashes, and I don't know if they were just coming on more that day, or if it was because I was stressing and straining not to open my mouth and tell my secret, but I made it through. I spent the night 'cause me and my sisters started talking and drinking that Dry Sack sherry. She brought out the special glasses, and we sat around and talked and laughed and told all of the kids and grandkids stories about our childhood experiences. We even pulled out some old pictures of our parents, who are long gone. The teenage kids were all upstairs on the east side of the house. They had music going, videos, games, Wii, Xbox 360, Connect, and you name it, they had it! They all had iPhones and iPads. They carry designer purses, wear designer coats and shoes. You name it, they had it!

I wondered what they would think if they knew their great auntie had all this money. Well, it would come out soon, because once I told their grandmothers, my sisters, you know they were gonna share their money with their family and tell it all! That's why they are so spoiled now. You know there is nothing like a grandmother's love. All the brothers-in-law were in the cave. That's what they call it; it's way on the opposite side of the house from where we were. I guess they had fun too. We only heard from them once. My sister's husband called on the intercom and asked if she would bring all of them some desert and some corn whiskey from the wine cellar. That was around nine p.m., and we never heard any more from them after that.

I said my goodbye to everyone and headed home. I enjoyed hanging out with all of my sisters together at my big sister's house, but ain't nothing like sleeping in your own bed and that's exactly what I planned to do when I got home. Relax and watch some Lifetime. Tomorrow I would call Ms. J to see if she has my travel present ready for those book club girls.

I made it a little early. My sister gave me so much food to bring home, I wouldn't have to cook for a week. I could eat as much as I wanted, and when I got tired of it, I'd feed it to Butch, my neighbor's dog. He just loved me; I fed him all the time. Whenever I was in the yard tending to my flowers, he just followed me along the fence wagging his tail. He almost looked as if he was smiling and saying, "I know your secret, I see you planting that money, but I'll never tell, 'cause you're so good to me." But you know a dog can't talk. Just a little funny saying I remember that my mom used to say when she was telling me a story as a kid, or I should say, one of the many stories she would tell.

I was eager to run a hot bath and relax, but the first thing I did after I disarmed the alarm system was to check my telephone for voice messages. I saw the light blinking and wondered which girlfriend called me this time. Who needed to borrow money? It wasn't any girlfriend, though. It was Ms. Jellory. Her message said, "Sorry it took me so long to get back with you, Ms. G., but I've finally completed your travel arrangements, and I think you will be pleased. Give me a call at your earliest convince and we can discuss the itinerary. You can pick them up or I'll be happy to deliver them personally to you."

The book club meeting was in two weeks, so I went ahead and called her.

She answered right away. "How about if I come by Friday, say around one p.m. That's when I usually take my lunch, and I'll just make my lunch hour with you."

"Sounds good, Baby, and don't bring any food. I've got plenty!"

Hum, I thought. Butch might get mad at me. I know Ms. J. is a big girl, but I don't think she'll eat up all the food I've got. I'll just make sure I leave some for Butch.

Before I knew it, it was Friday, exactly one week from the girls' next book club meeting. Ms. Jellory got to my house at exactly one p.m. She's such a bubbly girl. She came in with her brief case, kinda basic if you ask me. I decided I'd give her a new brief case for Christmas, along with some money. She never complains, but I know she's struggling. She's a single mom with two jobs. I'd make sure to get her name engraved on her briefcase as well.

"What do you think, Ms. G.?" she asked, handing me the itinerary.

My, my, this was gonna be some trip:

Party of ten, non-stop service to Los Angeles

First class

Delta Flight 256:

Departing ST, 11:15 a.m./Arriving LAX, 3:45 p.m.

Delta Flight 711:

Departing LAX, 6:00 p.m./Arriving LSV, 6:45 p.m.

Delta Flight 747:

Departing LSV, 4:55 p.m./Arriving ST, 8:50 p.m.

Leisure Travel Limo Service–LAX to Shorefront Properties, Malibu Beach (two condos; maximum occupancy 10)

Leisure Travel Limo Service—Shorefront Properties, Malibu Beach to LAX for departure on Delta Airlines

Exotic Limo Service—LSV to Wynn Hotel, Las Vegas

Exotic Limo Service—Wynn Hotel, Las Vegas to LSV

1. Limo Service to be utilized for entire three weeks on as needed basis

2. Travel dates open; tickets are valid for 1 year from date of purchase

3. Three month advance reservation required for Shorefront Properties

4. Three month advance reservation required for limo service in Los Angeles

5. Forty-eight hour reservation required for limo service in Las Vegas

6. All tips and gratuities included

"Oh, Baby," I said, "I know they are gonna love it. I can't wait to give it to them. Let's eat lunch."

We ate; she ate a lot and then, she left.

My next decision was what to put these presents in. I decided to make individual cards. No, I'd put them all in one big box with separate envelopes inside. I would number each one from one to ten, except my baby's envelope; I'd put her name on hers. What a pleasure it's been, just to be able to give so freely. I was so happy that I didn't have to loan money and have people pay me back with that look in their eyes. That look that says, "I am giving it back as promised, but I really am in need of keeping it." So, I was gonna bless as many people that I could who I felt deserved and would appreciate it. Which is most of my friends that I've been in contact with everyday for most of my life, except now, they didn't know, didn't have a clue, that I was a lotto winner! I had millions! Yeah!

I called Becky after the travel agent left and told her to come by and pick up the present I had for her and her girlfriends in the book club.

"Okay, mom, I've been running around so much, but I'll get there between now and Wednesday of next week."

"Okay, just call me first. I do go places sometime."

When I got off the phone, it hit me. I still had to go and get it wrapped. I needed to go to the bank and get cashier's checks for each of them. She goes to her meeting on Friday. I would go to First Tennessee on Monday. I love First Tennessee; they always made me feel like a big shot at that bank, whenever I came in. All the tellers, everyone who works there, knew me. The bank manager always acknowledged me when I come in, too, with, "Hey Ms. Ghoston. How you doing today?"They would lay out red carpet when I entered if they knew about my secret. Haven't quite figured out what bank or where I want to deposit that check yet. For now, I'll just leave it in my safe. I'm spending my money that I've had sitting in the bank for all of these years. When I got to First Tennessee, I asked the teller, "Are you ready to get a headache, Baby? I have quite a few transactions."

She said, "Oh Ms. Ghoston. It's never a headache helping you."

"I want to get nine cashier's checks at five thousand each and one more for ten thousand. Now can you do that? I don't know each of their full names."

"Well, I've never had a request for cashier's checks without a name assigned. I'll have to ask the manager." When she returned she said, "Ms. Ghoston, the bank only issues cashier's checks when you have a designated payee."

"Oh, no; now what am I going to do?"

"Well, Ms. Ghoston, let me think about this for a minute. You say it's Christmas presents, and you don't have the full name for each person? Then just give them American Express gift cards. That would be your best bet. It's covered just in case it's lost or stolen; it can be used for any kind of purchase anywhere; plus, they can get cash if they choose."

"Okay, you know what's best," I agreed.

"Can you have a seat for me in the waiting area and I'll bring everything over to you once I'm done? This is going to take a little time, so please be patient with me. Did you say you wrote everything down?"

"Yes. Here, take my list."

A few minutes went by and she came over to me speaking very low. She said, "Could you go over this list one more time to make sure I have it right?

"Sure, let's see, nine American Express Gift Cards for five thousand each, one American Express Gift Card for ten thousand, and one cashier's check made out to Jellory Scurlark for five thousand. Yes, Baby, you have that exactly right."

"Thanks, Ms. Ghoston. Can I get you some water or coffee while you wait?"

"Well, yes. I'll take some water, thank you."

The teller brought my bottled water. I got comfortable as I sat there watching the news. The television was on Channel 9 News. I sat there and watched TV as she prepared my gifts. I withdrew a total of sixty thousand. I saw the looks from the other tellers and the bank manager. They'd never seen me come in and get this amount of money at one time. Last time I needed a lump sum of money was when I came to get just about the same amount of money to purchase my Lexus five years ago.

I sat there patiently. I thumbed through a few magazines, and then, I heard it, and so did everyone else in the bank. They were talking on TV about the person who won the Powerball for $281,000,000. They said the person finally came forward to claim the winnings. They announced that it was an unknown woman. They talked about how she came into the lotto office in Nashville and stated she knew she had 180 days to claim her prize and that she'd planned and chose to come in on the 179th day, and that she also requested to remain anonymous. It seemed as if everyone in the bank froze. They couldn't believe it. Everyone had comments. One person said, "About time someone in Tennessee won. We've been playing for so long and people win in some strange place like Minot, Minnesota. About time."

Someone else said, "How could she do it? I don't think I could've kept it to myself that long."

Someone replied, "Kept it to myself? I would've gotten my money right away."

Another person said, "She must already have money. Ain't no way my broke behind could've waited for 179 days. Do you realize that's right at six damn months! Wow. Wonder who she was."

I wanted to jump up and run out of that bank, but I just sat there and on the inside my heart was skipping a beat! No one knew it was me. Once the news reporters started discussing the weather, the people in the bank changed their conversations over to that, and I was glad. The teller showed up and said, "Here you go, Ms. Ghoston. Thank you for banking with us and have a Merry Christmas."

Whew! I was glad to be out of that bank, surprised I didn't have a hot flash, but for some reason, it didn't hit me that time. I stopped at Dillard's and bought some of those pre-decorated boxes. I got three. You never know who I might need a box for, this way I'd have it and wouldn't hafta go back to the store again. I got in and out of that store in a flash. When I got home and relaxed, I opened the box that I'd picked for them. It was about the size of one of my hat boxes. That should be quite misleading. They would never know what was in store for them until they opened it. The bank gave me envelopes to put each gift card in, so I numbered them. I didn't write the numerical number but I spelled them out—one, two, three, four, five, six, seven, eight, nine, and the last one said Becky (ten). I put them all in the same box, taped it up, and sat it under my tree. I knew I wouldn't see Becky until Thursday, if not Friday, the day of their meeting. I'm just glad I got it done. The one thing I forgot to ask Ms. Jellory was to make sure these tickets are for a group, so no one will try to go without the other. I thought to also make sure to tell my daughter that when she comes by. No, I decided. I wasn't gonna say a word to her. That might give my secret away. That'd give me a reason to stop by the travel agency and give Ms. Jellory her Christmas present. I'd do that tomorrow. Today was just Wednesday, and Christmas was one week away. When I went out tomorrow, I would find Ms. Jellory the brief case I want for her and put her cashier's check inside.

The next day, I stopped by William Sonoma and found the perfect brief case for her and swung by the agency to drop off her present. I got there just in time. They were preparing to close.

Ms. Jellory looked up from her desk, surprised to see me. She asked, "Did I forget something? What did I leave off?"

"No, no, I brought something for you."

I handed her a gift wrapped in beautiful blue foil with white snow flakes on it. She was so happy from the commission she'd made off the itinerary she did for me, she thanked me again. She said her daughter would have a nice Christmas now.

I was glad; it makes me sad to watch a single mother struggle so hard. I didn't know what colors she liked so I got her a tan brief case, slid the money inside where they have little stretch strips to hold stuff. My card said, "To: Ms. J., Merry Christmas to my favorite travel agent. From: Ms. G."

I made her promise not to open her present until Christmas. She was shaking the box and I kept saying, "No, no, you're hurting my box."

She finally stopped and said, "Thanks Ms. G., and Merry Christmas to you, too."

As I was driving home from the agency, my daughter Becky called. She said, "Hey, Mom, where are you"

I told her, "You don't ask grown folks where they at."

She laughed, "I'm trying to come over and pick up the present you got for the book club. I know if I don't get it today, I will be pressed for time tomorrow 'cause we're exchanging gifts and I still hafta get the person's gift whose name I pulled. I got Renee's name and I don't know what to get her. She's got just about everything."

"I'll be home in the next thirty minutes. If you get there first use your key. Otherwise, I'll see you when you get here."

"Okay, Mom. Hum, I know what I can get Renee. I will go by that African shop in the mall run by that boy who has the dreads in his hair. I bet he can get me what I want for her. I will get her a nice quantity of real shea butter, and a gift certificate for a massage at Gould's. That'll work."

A few minutes later, Becky came through the door. "Hi, Mom. Mom, where are you?"

I was in the house playing a CD and playing it really loud. "Mom, you're too old to be listening to R. Kelly."

"I don't think so. Now go look under the tree and get the box with the big red, green and white bow. That's for you and the book club girls. I sure hope they like it. You tell them all I said Merry Christmas."

"I will, Mom."

She picked up the box and shook it a little. She smiled at me.

"Wow, the neighborhood still looks good. It still looks the same after all these years. It's just like when I was growing up. Everyone still keeps up with one another and all the yards still look good. I see they still have the contest for best yard decorated at Christmas, and as I remember, you always win."

"Becky, are you gonna stay awhile or do you have to go?"

"Why, Mom? Are you rushing me?"

"No, just asking. I want to get my gown on and relax and watch me some Lifetime."

"Now, I know you're gonna try to make me eat something, but I am saving up for the book club's Christmas celebration tomorrow. I thought I'd check my email and then I'm leaving. I hafta try to catch the person I need to get that Christmas gift for, Renee. We've been playing phone tag all day."

"Okay, Baby, take your time. I'm going in the back to get out of these clothes."

Becky was on the computer when I came back out. "What is that man of yours getting you for Christmas?"

"I don't know. I've been sending hints his way and asking for an iPad and something by Chanel. I guess I'll just have to wait and see. I got you something, Mom, but I will give it to you when you come over for dinner at Christmas. You will be there, right?"

"Yes, Baby, I'll be there."

"Okay Mom. I'm finished checking my email and I am gonna head on home. By the way, why do you have so many Poinsettias?"

"Oh, I am giving them out to the homeless people down at the union mission. I'm supposed to help serve food. Everyone always gives them food but never think about giving them a flower.

Becky looked curious, then she smiled at me. "Oh, okay, that's nice, Mom. I'll call you and let you know how the book club girls like their present from you. Love you."

"Okay, Baby, love you too! See you later."

What she didn't know is in each one of those poinsettias is a one-hundred dollar bill.

I know my daughter and those girlfriends of hers are going to have a screaming fit when they open that present from me. I wish, like the old folks used to say, that I could be a fly on that wall.

BECKY

I was thinking about my mom on the way to the book club Friday evening. She tells me she's okay, and she has plenty of friends, family, and associates to keep her busy. So I let her live her life. Some of my friends try to control what their parents do now that they are older, but as long as she's not sick… She's okay and if she really needed me, she would let me know.

Got to the book club meeting on time, as scheduled. Everyone was pulling in back to back. We all looked good. Everybody had on red, green, or winter white and black. My girls, we all loved to look good and have a good time. I knew everyone would be dressed in those same kind of colors underneath as well. Everyone seemed happy. Everybody had boxes, bags, you name it. We were all in the Christmas spirit, and guess what? All of the guys were dressed in Santa suits, so you couldn't tell who was who. What a trip. This was gonna be some night. First we did our ritual. Then, the party began! The guys served us drinks and their Christmas presents to us. The presents from the guys were all the same for each of us. I won't say exactly what they were, but I'll say, we'll never have any dry nights if we use them... hmm. I bet that was Ms. Phyllis's idea. The velvet drawstring pouches that our presents were in had *The Book Club* embroidered on them.

Then, we exchanged gifts amongst each other. We had all the old school Christmas music playing, and as usual, Ms. Phyllis outdid herself. The house was beautiful. The tree decorations were red, white, and green. Phyllis said it was ten feet tall, a Noble Fir tree. She had it special delivered from Oregon and brought in on Amtrak.

They didn't know it, but Ms. Phyllis had presents from each of us for our guests, a money clip with a thousand dollar bill attached to it. We do know they all really like money!

Then Foy, as usual, said, "Let's get this party started!" We had a champagne fountain flowing, herbal stuff burning, cigars smoking, the finest chocolates for eating, and it was on! We had crystal and china everything. Everybody was mingling well and slowly going their separate ways when I remembered the present from my mom.

"Wait, wait, we have one more present," I yelled, "It's from my mom."

Renee said, "Oh, Lord. What? She sent us a new book to read?"

Somebody else said, "No, she probably sent us all a subscription to Grace Magazine."

We laughed and I said, "I have no clue. Let's open it and see."

Yolanda said, "Yeah, y'all, we need to let Becky open it since it's from her momma."

Ms. Phyllis stepped in and said, "No, let's have a drink first, y'all. I want to make a toast and then we are gonna flip a coin. Heads, I open it, and tails Becky opens it."

Everyone agreed. We opened a bottle of Moët & Chandon champagne that was in the crystal ice bucket at the wet bar and we all got a glass. We passed the bottle around and poured. We raised our glasses and Phyllis said, "Merry Christmas to the baddest bitches I know this side of Nashville, Tennessee."

Everyone said, "Hear, hear! Merry Christmas."

We all sipped our champagne and Phyllis flipped the coin. It was tails, so I got to open the box. Inside the box was a big card that said, "Merry Christmas to the ones I love."

When I opened the card, ten envelopes fell out with the numbers from one to ten written in words. In the envelope with ten, it said, "To my daughter, Becky."

Foy opened hers first. She screamed, "Yeah! Yeah! Yeah!"

It was plane tickets and a small white envelope. Everyone started opening theirs as well. Each of them got a gift card for five thousand dollars, along with plane tickets for Los Angeles and Las Vegas. Everybody looked at me and said, "Becky, did your momma hit the Jackpot or what!"

"If she did, she didn't tell me. You know, she always goes to that casino with her senior citizen girlfriends. Let me open mine."

It said, "I love you, Baby. Merry Christmas."

Inside, I also had plane tickets and a gift card, except mine was for ten thousand.

Everyone started dancing and talking and partying and comparing their tickets and gift cards. In my head, I thought, "My Mom's got some explaining to do. Where did she get all of this money?"

We didn't rush off to separate rooms, the way we usually did. Instead, we partied with all of the Santas. We danced, drank, and laughed.

Yolanda said, "I nominate myself to coordinate the trip. I want everyone to check their calendars and see when we can all get time off together to make this happen. Let's say, next meeting we all bring dates when we're available."

We were all dancing and swaying our hips to the song, *This Christmas*, by Donny Hathaway. I just couldn't get over it. Where did my mom get all of this money? Who put this together for her? I'm gonna talk to her at Christmas dinner; she's been keeping some secrets from me. I looked around and a few of us had disappeared. A few Santa's were missing as well. I knew what that meant. It was party time.

I passed Foy and she said, "I just love the book club. This is how a girl is supposed to have fun."

Then I remembered, "Oh, damn! Ms. Phyllis. We forgot to give her present."

We had all put in and purchased her a new car. She had just about rode the tires off that Volkswagen Jetta. Yolanda's husband owned a car lot, so we all got together and purchased her a new 370Z, black on black, convertible top, fully loaded. I started looking for Phyllis and calling her. She was nowhere to be found. Something said, "Check down in the sitting room on the lower level." She likes to go there and watch TV. Sometime she's in there knitting something. The girl is bad. She makes sweaters, blankets, blouses, everything. I told her she should sell them, but she said she does it as a hobby only. Guess what she was doing? She had let Rainbow, the limo driver, in and they were getting pretty busy.

"Oh damn," I thought, but interrupted her anyway, "Excuse me, ma'am, but you didn't get your Christmas present from us."

"I'm trying to get my Christmas present now."

"I see that. I promise you this will only take a second. Can you excuse us for a minute, Rainbow?"

He was grinning. The room was dark and he's as dark as night. All I could see was teeth. He had such pretty white teeth.

We went back to the great room where we all just left and I couldn't find nobody. I said, "I'm sorry Phyllis, looks like everybody's busy."

"Yeah, including me," she said.

"I'll just hafta give it to you and you can tell us later how you like it."

"Okay, okay. Now go. I'm having fun."

"Phyllis, we didn't forget you, and we love you. You have been keeping us happy all year and we just want to show our appreciation."

I gave her the box and she hurriedly opened it. It was a pair of black shoes. She said, "Thanks, girl, and I'll tell the others later."

"Open the box, and try them on."

"Becky, I love y'all, but we are all fucked up. Can't I try them on later?"

"Hell, no."

"Alright, but these better be some damned amazing shoes."

She sat down on the chaise lounge and took a good look at what she had. She said, "What, you shitting me, a pair of pumps by Christian Louboutin, red bottoms?"

"I hope we got your size right. Try them on."

She put the left shoe on first. When she tried to put her foot in the right shoe, she said, "Ouch, something's in this one."

She took off the one shoe, stood up kinda wobbly, and reached her hand inside it. She started crying loud and that made everyone come out of their spot. "No, y'all didn't," she shrieked. "Where is it? Where is it?" she said, running in circles.

"It's parked in the garage, girl," Valerie told her.

She ran to the garage and started screaming, "I knew y'all were my kind of girls. I love it. Love the shoes, too."

Jernethia told her, "Give your Jetta to your grandson. He loves to work on cars. He can fix it up and drive it 'cause you don't need it anymore. We got you some new wheels, Baby!"

"Can I drive it home tonight?"

"It's yours, dawg! Feel free," Faye said.

"Merry Christmas, Phyllis, you deserve it!" Jessica told her. "But we don't suggest you or any of us drive tonight."

I opened another bottle of champagne and we started partying all over again. When I finally looked at the time it was midnight and everybody was toasted, including the limo driver. We all took a look at one another and said, "Let's make it an all-nighter!"

"That's what I'm talking about," said Foy, "That's Christmas."

This would be the first night we actually had the guys stay over, and they didn't seem to mind, especially since they got a one thousand dollar money clip for Christmas. That was like getting paid for overnight service. We each got with our special Santa and everyone disappeared to their designated places. Ms. Phyllis said, "I will call home for everyone. Merry Christmas!"

SARA

Becky's house was decorated beautifully. The outside had the clear twinkling lights, and she had four reindeer in the front yard. They were so pretty. You know, the ones that move their heads. She has the icicle lights, just beautiful. They were hanging on the house, from the roof all the way around the sides. She also had twinkling lights leading around her beautiful spiral driveway. I am so proud of her. She seems to be doing well with that husband of hers. And my granddaughter is getting to be quite a beautiful young lady. They have the cutest little dog named Cupcake, just a little bit too hyper for me. I babysat her one time. She got away from me and was chasing and charging at Butch, my big dog friend that lives in back of me. I almost had a massive coronary, 'cause I knew my grandbaby would've just died if something happened to that little dog of hers.

When I rang the doorbell, I could hear her coming down the stairs. She opened the door and I immediately smelled the balsam candles burning. She had the stairs decorated with white poinsettias that had silver and green accessories. What a beautiful sight. Her tree was huge. I don't know how she gets it up and decorates that big thing by herself every year. I must say, it looked good.

"Well, well. Merry Christmas, Mom," my handsome son-in-law was coming toward me from his study.

He gave me a hug and kiss on the cheek as usual. "Mom, your daughter outdid herself this time. She's got the house looking good and the food, I mean, she…she…the food tastes good, too. Aw, I've been sneaking a few bites in here and there all day when she's not looking. Say, I just have to read a few more e-mails and I'll be right back. Then, I promise no more work."

I thought to myself, "He's always working. I don't think he knows how to not work," but I waved him off.

I could smell the food, and when I entered the dining room, it was how a dining room is supposed to look. The table was set for ten. "Where is Paris?" I asked.

"Oh, she's upstairs in her room, you know she's showing out. Her cousins are here."

"Well, I know I'm a little early. You said four, and it's just three-thirty now."

"Mom, you can come anytime, you know that."

"Yes, I do, but I don't like to get in young folks' way."

"Well, I just hafta put the rolls in the bread warmer. Then, we can eat. Now, Mom, since I got you all to myself right now, let me tell you, the girls at the book club loved their presents! They are so ready to go, and me too. We plan to discuss times and dates at the next meeting. Thanks, Mom. You know, that was quite an expensive gift. Did you win the lottery or hit a jackpot at the casino or something?"

"Now, Baby, you know, I don't do much money spending anymore, and I save a lot more since you got married."

"Ha, Ha. Funny, Mom."

"Well, it's true and you know it. No, I just thought I'd use some of my savings since it's Christmas. Can't I be in the giving mood?"

"Well, you blew us all away."

"Just say, 'thank you, Mom' and stop reading more into it, okay?"

"Okay, Okay, but, Mom, you sure you ain't got some secret going on that you need to tell me?"

"Girl, please…let's eat. I'm hungry. Did you make some chitterlings?"

"Yes, Mom, just for you."

"That's my baby. Now what time is your sister coming, and where are those aunts of yours?"

"That's why I said four, 'cause then they may make it on time by five."

"Okay. I'm gonna give them exactly until five and then I'm gonna eat. I don't care if no one ain't here."

By the time I got that sentence out of my mouth, the doorbell started ringing and everyone was coming in. I think they must've all met at the entrance gate, lined up, and drove in like a caravan. My people, we got all kinds and you just gotta love 'em. After dinner, we all sat around the fireplace, kids playing, people talking, movies going, dog running around, people having drinks, music playing, and people eating deserts. What a great day.

I stayed until most everyone had gone and then I told Becky my plan so she could tell her sister. "Baby," I said, "I'm glad you and those girls liked your Christmas present. I'm gonna get ready to go now. I've been over here all day.

"Oh, Mom. It's only nine-thirty."

"Becky, honey, I've got to get up early in the morning."

"Why? Where are you going, Mom?"

"I'm gonna catch some after Christmas sales."

"I'll go with you if you want me too," Becky offered.

"No thanks, but I do need you to do me a little favor."

"Okay, what?"

"I'll let you know tomorrow. Now give me a hug so I can get on home. Old lady has been out long enough."

I had asked Ms. Jellory to put a little travel package together for me as well. When I got home, which only took twenty minutes from Becky's house, I finished my packing. I packed light; I planned on buying whatever came to mind for me that I wanted when I got to wherever I wanted. I got my shower, put on my comfortable pajamas, and took a look around the house. I also looked at my dear husband's picture. I thought, "Ben, I wish you were here to share this blessing with me."

I kissed his picture, sat it back on my night stand, set my clock for five-thirty a.m. and went to bed with a smile on my face. I woke up on the first ring of my alarm. I was ready to go. I got out of the house by six-fifteen, and drove straight to my daughter's house. It was still dark when I pulled up in the driveway. I left the car running and sat the envelope at the door. Then, I headed straight for the airport. My flight was scheduled to depart at eight a.m.

I had put together a planner for Becky with detailed instructions on keeping my flowers watered, the telephone number for the contractor that's coming out first of the year to build the green house, and a few names of people whose addresses I wanted her to get for me.

I also left a note explaining my situation and it went kinda like this:

Becky,

I will be traveling around for a while but I will eventually return. Go ahead and feel free to call everyone. That means your aunts, uncles, and the whole family, including my sisters and brothers, as well as anyone else that you want to know about my windfall. I love you. Tell everyone in the family, as well as my friends, that I love them all, too, and to watch the mail, because I WILL BE IN TOUCH!

Love always,

Your Momma

I enclosed a picture of me that I had to take holding that sign, that damn sign with the caption, "Sara Ghoston, Powerball Jackpot Winner—$281 Million."

BECKY

It's a new year now and I haven't heard a word from anyone since we got tore down at the Christmas meeting. Guess everyone had a good Christmas and New Year. This will be our first meeting of the New Year, and I hope everyone remembered that we have business to take care of. We were all so tore down. What a night! Shit was everywhere. The guys were all gone by the time we got up the next morning, thank God, because Yolanda's husband decided to come by to check on us. When he got there Saturday morning, we were all up having breakfast. No sign of any uninvited guest. Just a girl thang going on as usual.

A few of us were in the Jacuzzi. He could see them from the great room when he entered the house. He felt out of place and could feel the vibes from the rest of us for invading our space. We wondered why in the hell he felt the need to bust up out here to check on his wife like she was a kid. Nobody had anything to say. He spoke to Yolanda and then quickly left.

Everybody had a hangover, and it felt kinda strange knowing that Rose was out there somewhere, but no longer a member of the book club. We were so used to her going overboard and causing some kind of major drama. Strange, but good in a way.

Today, it was time for us to handle our unfinished business. We were to decide who we would allow to take Rose's place, as well as when we would have our fun trip.

Everybody had their calendars out and we got started.

"I think June would be a great month for the trip," Yolanda said.

"It's really hot that time of year in Las Vegas and Los Angeles," Jernethia told her.

"Maybe August?" Renee offered.

"I don't know," I said. "I just know we are going and the sooner the better. Don't want everyone to start spending their gift cards on other stuff or other people."

Ms. Phyllis had scheduled our toys to come at nine p.m. instead of eight, so that we would have ample time to take care of everything. It was also time to pay our club dues. Jernethia brought the meeting to order. We did our ritual and got started.

"We've had a pretty nice winter. Not a lot of cold days, not a lot of snow. Just right, but it sure would be nice to go and get some sunshine on this body and I know I don't just speak for myself," I said. "Let me bring everyone up to date. The first news is, my mom won the lottery! Yay! Yeah, she was the person they were talking about on the news who hadn't come forward to claim her money. She planned it that way, waited until the 179th day to come forward. I had no idea. She's somewhere traveling now. I still can't believe it."

Everyone cheered.

"In other news, Yolanda got a partner for her dental practice. Renee is retiring after thirty years as an RN; Faye is having her first grandbaby; Jernethia won her federal lawsuit. Valerie won Principal of the year, Tennessee, Statewide. Jessica opened a fitness club, and Rose, Rose is doing fine. She said she will try to stop by tonight's meeting. She asked if it would be okay for her to bring Joann. She didn't want to take the drive out alone, it takes her about two hours to get here now. I didn't see a problem with it, so I told her okay."

I took a drink of water and continued, "Our book club is doing fine, and, after you ladies pay your yearly dues tonight, we should have total of $265, 000. When we take our trip and return, it will be time to retire some of our guys and make room for new. I think we have about three guys that will turn forty this year. Okay, now let me get y'all's money, and then I will shut up and turn it over to Yolanda. We are going to be five grand short because Rose is out. Would anyone like to make a motion that we each split the amount of Rose's yearly dues between us until we get a replacement? That would mean we each pay $5, 500 each, just this one time."

Foy said, "Umh!"

Everyone got quiet.

Then Faye said, "I think we should wait on that discussion. Let's see who we come up with for a replacement first."

Everyone agreed that was a good idea.

The doorbell rang, and who else, but Rose, entered, with Joann at her side.

I heard somebody say, "Did she really need to bring that thang with her? She ain't no member."

I think Rose felt the vibes 'cause she told Joann, "Go on out on the deck, Baby. I'll get with you in just a second."

They kissed and Joann turned and said, "Sure. Bye, y'all."

Renee had this smirk on her face as she was rubbing the back of her hair and looking off.

Mabel gave Renee a look." Hey, Rose, come on down.

I got back to business." All right, what about the new member?"

"I left mine in the box last time I was here," Jessica said.

Foy said, "I left mine in the box last year. Yeah, it was last year."

"All right, everyone else?"

Everyone who hadn't done so already wrote their nomination. The box was passed around the room and everyone else dropped theirs in.

"Okay," I said. "Which do we tackle first, the trip or the new member?"

Rose said, "Oh, maybe I should step out!"

"No, you don't hafta leave," Jessica said.

"Yeah, you been with us too long for that girl. Don't be acting like a stranger and shit!" Foy told her.

Valerie laughed." You ain't been gone that long, hefa."

Yolanda said, "Okay, this is how we're gonna do this. First Rose will call out all of the names from the box."

Rose started calling them out, "Mary Jane, Gina, Freda, Charlene, Tamika, Curtistene, Rochelle, Amira, and Eva."

Rose stopped suddenly, "Who nominated Eva? Eva who? Who named Eva?"

"Well, I did," Jessica said.

"What's her last name?"

"Halston."

Rose looked at me and back at Jessica," I didn't know you knew that bitch," she said.

"Hold on now. . ."

"That's the woman from the church that's been fucking my husband."

Then, Faye said, "Oh hell to the naw."

Jessica turned red. "Oh, God, Rose. I had no idea. But anyway, Eva called me up and told me she and her husband had worked things out, and she didn't want to be spending nights away from home."

Rose rolled her eyes.

It got quiet in the room. Then Faye said, "I suggested Mary Jane. She has wanted to join for years now. You know she's the interior decorator that fixed up the place. She knows a little about us already. Maybe she would make a good fit."

"I suggested Curtistine," Yolanda said, "because she recently divorced her husband and she ain't no spring chicken anymore. She's pretty financially stable."

"And I suggested Rochelle. She's not from Tennessee. She relocated here with her husband who retired from the military after 34 years. She's from Albany, New York," Mabel said.

Foy said, "Hell! This is too damned hard, and sorry, ladies, but y'all are about to cut into my fun time. We have one hour to wrap this shit up or we're gonna hafta take it to next meeting. A girl like me," she got up and started shaking her butt, "just wanna have fun."

"Sit your ass down!" Faye and Yolanda said in unison. "We gonna finish this shit tonight."

Then out of the blue, Rose said, "A new friend could bring our best kept secret to an end."

"Damn straight," Foy said, "We don't hafta replace Rose, 'cause we all know there will never be another like you, girl."

Yolanda said, "Then that settles it! No replacement."

"Not now. Not never," Foy said, "Ha. Ha. Now can we move on?"

Valerie had been quiet for a little while, listening to the exchange. She cleared her throat a little bit. "Um, ya'll, I have something I need to tell you."

We all looked over at her unexpectedly.

"My old friend, Dennis is selling his club, and he's moving back to Memphis. We're going to try making it work together. The book club has been one of the best things in my life, but I think I'm ready to move on."

It was deathly silent for a moment, then we all began to talk at once.

"You're serious?"

"Oh, my God, girl. I'm so happy for you!"

"Have you fucking lost your ever-lovin' mind?"

We all laughed, and hugged Valerie.

I finally got everybody to quiet down. "All right, ya'll. I have a suggestion. No replacement for Rose, as we agreed. But I say, let's offer Valerie's place to Phyllis. What do you think?"

"It's perfect, but can she afford it?"

"Well, I was thinking. Phyllis does so much to keep things running smoothly here. How about we waive the initiation, and half her annual fees, and absorb the difference? We've got enough in the kitty to easily do that."

Everyone agreed on that.

"Okay, who wants to begin giving me dates they suggest for our trip?" Yolanda asked. "And Rose and Valerie, you have to be in on this. You both have tickets, after all."

Valerie said, "I can get away mid-March over Spring Break, or in June when school lets out."

Mabel offered, "I'd like to go when it's hot, 'cause I'm always cold. I was thinking May or June."

I told her, "I can't tell, you seem pretty warm to me when you get to this here book club."

"Ha, ha, Becky, but you got a point."

"I don't care when we go," Foy said, "Let's just go! Let's do the damned thing! Everybody here is grown and able to go whenever they please. We ain't got no babies and our husbands can babysit themselves. You hefas with businesses got partners or staff and assistants and shit. So let's make it happen."

"Okay," Yolanda said, "So far we have March or June. Let's take five. It's eight thirty and our toys will be here in thirty minutes."

Some of us refilled our drinks while others freshened up. Others got some of the food that Phyllis had prepared—crab cakes, shrimp cocktail, asparagus dip. Renee stepped out to get her a little toke.

When we came back, it was the same chaos all over again. Then Faye said, “Hell. It doesn’t matter. Let Becky pick.”

Everyone nodded their heads, so I said, “Let's go in March.”

Yolanda asked, “Can everybody work with that?”

Everyone agreed.

“Whew. That’s settled. I'll have more details next meeting.”

That’s when I heard the garage door opening. “Where is Foy?” I asked. “Foy?”

“What's the word?” she said. “Let's get this party started!”

YOUR SECRET TENNESSEE

Now, how many secrets do you have? How many times in your life have you pleaded with someone, "Please, keep it a secret?"

How many times has someone said to you, "Don't tell nobody. I haven't told no one this secret but you. So please, please, don't tell nobody!"

And, how many times has that secret been so damn juicy, hot, scandalous that you just had to tell it to one somebody, even though you promised not to tell? It always comes out, regardless. Regardless of who you are or where you live. It comes out while you're alive or it damn sure comes out once you're dead! You know, there are a few people who can, and will truly keep what you say a secret if you ask them to, and never tell a soul, but most people won't!

Do you know why? Let me tell you why. 'Cause the real secret is there ain't no secrets! There's always somebody who knows somebody, who knows somebody, who knows your secret!

END